“Roni—”

“Mark. Don’t.” She had to stop him. She had to stop him before he asked her for something she couldn’t give. Before he demanded the truth. “What we have is perfect.” She even leaned in and kissed him, to make her point.

“Is it?”

It was perfect for her. She was blissfully happy for the first time in her life. She didn’t want this to end.

She knew it wasn’t perfect for him. She’d known for a while. She’d sensed it. But she wasn’t ready to have *this* conversation. Not today. So she pulled her hand from his, smiled and said, “It’s getting late. I have to get to work, and so do you.”

His stark expression crumpled into a wash of emotion. There was frustration in there. She could see it. “To hell with work, Roni,” he growled. “Nothing is as important to me as you are. Do you understand that? I love you. I want to be *with* you.”

“You are with me.” She cupped her hands around his face. “We’re together nearly every night.”

He shook his head. “I want more. Don’t you want more, Roni? Don’t you want a happy-ever-after?”

Dear Reader,

I am very happy to welcome you to the second Stirling Ranch adventure. This story comes from a very emotional corner of my heart. Though the subject matter is difficult for many, what I hope to share in this glimpse of renewal is that we can heal from hurt. And we can help heal each other. We need to.

In *Recipe for a Homecoming*, our heroine steps into the story having survived an abusive marriage. She is determined to be her own woman. She's not at all interested in having an intimate relationship with a man ever again. Mark is, therefore, effectively friend-zoned. The question is, can he prove to her that she can be her own woman and his at the same time?

INSIDE PEEK: Okay, confession time. Veronica, our heroine—or Roni, as Mark calls her—has a passion for baking. "Dang it, Sabrina," you say. "Why do you have so many bakers in your books?" I'm sure you can guess. The truth is, I like writing about pastries and éclairs and molasses cookies. Things I am not allowed to eat. Sigh.

At any rate, I hope you enjoy reading about how Mark and Veronica make their way back to love.

And for those of you who relate to Roni's story more than you'd like to, I'm sending you peace and love and, most of all, the strength to forgive and move on. It's your story now. Own it.

I'd love to hear your thoughts.

Check out all my books and contests at sabrinayork.com, and if you want to get updates about future books and tiara giveaways—and snag a free book—sign up for my newsletter at sabrinayork.com/gift.

Happy reading, my darlings!

Sabrina York

Recipe for a Homecoming

SABRINA YORK

ISBN-13: 978-1-335-40814-3

Recipe for a Homecoming

This edition published by arrangement with Harlequin Books S.A.

For questions and comments about the quality of this book, please contact us at CustomerService@Harlequin.com.

Harlequin Enterprises ULC
22 Adelaide St. West, 40th Floor
Toronto, Ontario M5H 4E3, Canada
www.Harlequin.com

Printed in U.S.A.

Sabrina York is the *New York Times* and *USA TODAY* bestselling author of hot, humorous romance. She loves to explore contemporary, historical and paranormal genres, and her books range from sweet and sexy to scorching romance. Her awards include the 2018 HOLT Medallion and the National Excellence in Romantic Fiction Award, and she was also a 2017 RITA® Award nominee for Historical Romance. She lives in the Pacific Northwest with her husband of thirty-plus years and a very drooly Rottweiler.

Visit her website at sabrinayork.com to check out her books, excerpts and contests.

Books by Sabrina York

Harlequin Special Edition

The Stirling Ranch

Accidental Homecoming

Visit the Author Profile page at Harlequin.com.

This book is dedicated to all my readers
who choose to look for the light.

Chapter One

"Well, it's official. You're the last man standing," Cole Taylor said, lifting his beer in Mark Stirling's direction. Laughter rounded the small living room of Mark's cabin, causing the dogs to start howling, too.

Mark loved the "puppers" he fostered until a forever home came along, but they were very easily led into howling. Especially when his boisterous friends came over to hang out for an evening.

Granted, they weren't as boisterous as they used to be, since Adam Scott owned a business, Ben Nadler was the bank manager and Cole was the deputy sheriff. Still, they managed to have a little bit of fun, even though it was limited to these poker games and the occasional volunteer firefighter trainings.

Adam shook his head as he shuffled the cards. "Who'da thunk it, back in high school? That *Nadler* would be engaged before Mark Stirling?"

"Hey!" Nadler exclaimed, shoving his glasses back up his nose.

But Adam was right. It was kind of unbelievable that Nadler found his *person* before him. Mark had always been the guy with a girlfriend—any girlfriend. But now… He blew out a breath and shook his head. Here he was, pushing thirty, available—and all his buddies were coupled up.

"Then again…" Adam chuckled. "It makes perfect sense. All the women in this town *know* you." The fact that the others laughed, too, made something sour swirl in his belly.

"Maybe I don't want to get married," he finally muttered, but that made them all collapse into more laughter. *Seriously?* "What's so funny?"

"Of course you don't want to get married." Adam pushed away from the table and headed for the fridge for another round of beers.

"Why would you?" Cole asked, as he popped open his brewski against the tabletop. "Aren't you living your best life? Why change?"

Nadler used the bottle opener, which Mark appreciated. The table wasn't fancy, but it deserved better than such abuse. "Face it, Stirling," he said. "The ladies love you."

Mark shrugged. He did have a pretty long history of dating just about every single woman in the county. Trouble was, he hadn't found anyone he wanted to be with on a more permanent basis. It wasn't so much a physical thing. It was just that all of his encounters left him wishing for something more. Something meaningful. Something…lasting.

Something…

Of course, Mark wasn't entirely sure what he was looking for to begin with. Happiness, certainly. But peace and an easygoing relationship appealed to him, as well. It was probably unrealistic to ask for more than that. Based on his experience, the ideal of a soul mate was a fantasy made up for reality TV.

His parents hadn't been great role models for connubial bliss. Though his mom had died when he was young, he still remembered the incessant fights between her and Pop reverberating through the house. They'd been far from lovey-dovey. And his grandfather—who'd taken on the task of raising the four Stirling kids when Pop died—had been about as romantic as a wart on a frog. So it probably made sense that none of his siblings had found true love, either. None of them knew what it looked like.

Danny, his half brother, was the only exception. He'd recently reunited with his long-lost love, Lizzie, and learned that he was a father, to an adorable munchkin named Emma, and the little family couldn't be happier. But then, Mark's newfound brother hadn't grown up on the ranch. Maybe that was the secret.

What did a happy relationship even look like, anyway? More to the point, what did *he* want a happy relationship to look like? Would he even recognize it if he saw it?

Snoopy, the newest addition to his menagerie,

nudged his arm and Mark responded by slipping him a pretzel, which the pup inhaled.

She'd have to love dogs. That was for certain.

"You'll never get married, man," Cole said as he surveyed his hand then rearranged his cards. "Why would a man settle for one woman when he can have them all?"

Mark snorted. "I hardly *have them all*." They weren't Pokémon, for pity's sake. "I haven't had a date in months." Maybe longer. He tried to remember the last woman he'd asked out, then realized it didn't matter who it was. He'd known, almost immediately, that she hadn't been what he was looking for. None of them were. And after that realization, it didn't make sense to continue dating at all.

It would help if he knew what he *was* looking for. But life was rarely that easy.

Adam sighed and slapped Mark on the back. "I guess you'll just be our single friend forever. Especially if you don't do anything about this pack of dogs you've got here."

"Now, hold on there!" Mark liked his friends. But that was a step too far. "The dogs are staying."

"Until they're adopted," Nadler reminded him. "That's what you said, right?"

Mark's gut lurched. The thought of having to give up his puppers—even to loving homes—and living here all alone was depressing. "Not all of them." At that moment, Snoopy hopped up on his lap, and even though the little rascal just wanted another pretzel, it made Mark feel better. There would always be homeless dogs, he told himself. He would never be totally alone.

A sharp knock on the door reminded him of the other reason he'd never be alone. It opened before he could answer, but Mark knew who it was. Shave-and-a-haircut was his sister Sam's trademark knock. Also, bursting in without an invitation—she was known for that, too.

While Mark chose to live in one of the cabins on the family ranch designated for crew who had families—and only a few currently had families—Sam lived up in the big house with their brother DJ, Danny and his family, Lizzie and Emma, as well as their grandma Dorthea. It wasn't that Mark didn't like living with his family. *They* didn't like living with his dogs. So he'd moved out here and after a while, he'd just come to prefer the privacy. This option was perfect for everyone.

Sam marched in with a huge, innocent smile on her face, which was misleading. Anyone who knew her knew there was nothing innocent about her. "Oh, hey, guys! Playing poker?" she asked gustily.

Adam covered up the pot with his hands. "You can't play."

Her big smile faded. "Why not? Are you guys afraid to lose…again?"

Adam grumbled a bit in response, but it was true.

Sam did have a tendency to come out ahead every time she played with them. They'd never figured out her poker face—they were probably tired of losing to her.

She grinned at Adam's sulky expression. "I understand," she said silkily. "You big strong men are afraid to play against a gal like me." She even batted her lashes.

But these guys had known her their entire lives. They were not fooled by her ploys.

"You know," Nadler said, scraping together what chips he had left, "I'd better be getting home. It's late."

"Oh, yeah," Sam said. "You'd better get home before Suzy starts calling around. Oh, by the way," she said, her tone turning genuine. "Congratulations, Nadler. I know you guys will be really happy together."

"Thanks, Sam," he said, smiling at her while collecting his things.

"I should probably get going, too," Adam said.

Cole nodded and stood, as well. They all said their goodbyes and headed out after Nadler.

Mark turned to Sam with a frown after everyone had left. "You sure do know how to break up a party."

She waved her hand dismissively. "It's a gift."

"Why did you come over?" he asked as he started cleaning up.

"I wanted to talk to you about something."

He paused. Glanced at her. Something in her tone was…concerning. “Is Emma okay?” Danny’s six-year-old daughter was recovering from a serious illness and had required a bone-marrow transplant to save her life. They all still worried about her, even though she was seven months postprocedure and the resultant treatments had been a success. In fact, she seemed to have more energy nowadays than all of them put together. There were just a few more boxes to tick before she’d be fully cleared.

“Emma’s fine.”

“Is it Lizzie?” Now that she was pregnant again, she’d been having morning sickness.

Sam blew out a breath that fluffed up her bangs. “Everyone is fine. I just wanted to talk to you.”

Oh, ugh. He knew that tone. Mark grimaced and flopped onto the sofa. The only girl born into a veritable herd of men, Sam had developed a strong personality and a stronger dislike for what she called the patriarchy, which, as far as he could tell, was any man doing anything she didn’t particularly like.

So *I just wanted to talk to you* wasn’t, generally, a welcome start to a conversation with Sam.

He frowned at her. “What?”

“Do you have any beer?”

Mark shrugged. “Check in the fridge.”

She did, focusing on the contents of his fridge as though they held the secrets of the Dead Sea Scrolls. After a full minute of surveillance, and several unappreciated *ews* and *yucks*, she grabbed a soda and came to the couch.

"You're out of beer." The moment she sat down, Snoopy jumped on her lap.

Traitor.

"Thanks for the update." Mark didn't add more, because it would be a waste of time to try to figure out what Sam wanted to say. It would also be a waste of time to ask her directly. She would take her time getting it out. She always did.

"So," she said after a long snort on her root beer. "Nadler's engaged."

"Yup."

They were silent for a moment, and then Mark added, "I'm the last man standing, I guess."

Sam nodded. "I never imagined Nadler would fall before you, but the one that really surprises me is Cole. How on earth did he ever find a woman who would tolerate his presence on a daily basis?"

"He's not that bad. Didn't you date him once?"

"Once." She rolled her eyes.

"So," Mark said, when his patience started to wane. "How was your day?"

Her smile unfurled, reminding him of the Grinch upon spotting a stocking to steal. "I went into town."

"Did you?" Why couldn't she just get to the point and tell him whatever juicy gossip she'd heard? Because *I went into town* was code for juicy gossip. At least, in this one-horse town.

"Mmm-hmm." She leaned back and Snoopy repositioned his long body across her lap, then rolled over, asking for a scratch. Without a thought, her fingers went to work. "I…ran into an old friend."

"Really?" An old friend? This was Butterscotch Ridge. Every friend was an old friend. And everyone knew everything about everybody. Even the stuff you didn't really care to know, like the fact that Gladys Henry had lumbago. *And* that she was having a secret affair with old Calvin Carter, who owned the pick-your-own apple orchard off the main highway.

"I did indeed." Sam tried to look all nonchalant, which set Mark's Spidey-senses a'tingling. "I was just wondering if you remembered her," she said as she took another swig of root beer.

Something prickled at his nape. "Sam, just tell me who you saw."

"Veronica James."

He nearly dropped his beer, which would have been a shame, because, apparently, it was the last one. "V-V-Veronica James?" Did he remember her?

Red hair, heart-shaped face, blossoming dimples when she smiled, sparkling green eyes and soft, sweet lips? And her laugh? It was contagious.

Did he remember her?

She'd been a huge part of his life when they were kids. She'd come every summer to visit her grandmother, Milly, who'd been their beloved housekeeper until she retired. They used to call her Aunt Milly. She'd practically raised them. Veronica would stay in the cabin her grandmother lived in, and come up to the main house every day to play with them. They'd had wild adventures, better than summer camp. Everything from swimming in the lake to creating elaborate cities for their Matchbox cars in the roots of the old oak in the yard, along with fishing, riding and sneaking goodies from the cooling rack in her grandmother's kitchen.

He'd kissed her once when he was sixteen. Maybe even fallen a little bit in love with her.

It was a damn shame that she hadn't come back the next summer. Or ever. How long had it been? More than a decade.

About four years ago, he'd seen Milly in town and while they were chatting, she told him Roni had gotten married. He'd been surprised at how much that fragment of information had hurt. But by then, it had been far too late to do anything about it. He had no one to blame but himself.

He'd had his chance, and he blew it.

But now she was back.

Married and back.

He tried to arrange his expression into something that resembled indifference. "She here for a visit?"

"She's here to stay with Milly for a while because Max and Gwen have been worried."

At this, he sat upright. Max and Gwen were Roni's cousins. They lived in town and had been taking turns looking after their grandmother. "Is Milly okay?" It alarmed him that she might be ill. And he hadn't known. Hadn't even asked. He should visit her more often...

Sam shook her head. "She's getting older. Max and Gwen wanted to put her into that place in Pasco."

"That place smells like disinfectant." He'd been to that nursing home, which was a nice old-fashioned name for what it was. He'd been there several times with his therapy dogs. He'd even convinced them to adopt some of the older animals he couldn't place elsewhere.

"Right. Roni didn't like the idea, either, so she agreed to come and stay with Milly. She's...assessing her, I guess."

Something stirred in his chest. "That was thoughtful." And then he asked, "Is she still teaching?" It was late spring. Would she leave when summer ended? She always had. Left when summer ended. The stirring in his belly turned sour.

"We didn't talk much. Lizzie and I just popped into Milly's store to say hello," she said as she took another sip.

Why the hell hadn't Sam found out more? Like where was her husband, the handsome doctor who'd won her heart? The man who'd had more than one adolescent kiss? Sam was an inveterate gossip hound. Surely she could have found out more.

Sam cleared her throat. "I'm sure she'd love to see you."

"Did she ask about me?"

"She did."

His heart leaped. Oh, that was good to hear—

"And Luke. And DJ." Sam's grin made clear she was tormenting him with the mention of his two annoying brothers. "She asked about *all* of us."

"Did she?" he grumbled.

"Mmm-hmm." Sam finished her root beer, gave Snoopy one last scratch, removed him from her lap and stood. "Well, that's my news."

"Thanks for telling me." His tone was hardly dry at all.

"No problemo." She walked to the door and turned back to send him one more irksome grin. "Sleep well," she said right before she let herself out—leaving him alone, with a room full of snoring dogs and the memories of a girl who'd made him feel so alive. A girl he'd never been able to forget.

He should stop by the bookstore Milly ran to say hello to her. And to Roni. She'd meant so much to him way back when… But then—with a bitter realization—he remembered that she was married, and he thought better of it. Seeing her again would be amazing. Meeting her husband—and pretending to be polite when he really wanted to punch the jerk—would be nothing short of galling. Better to just avoid her.

And, somehow, he convinced himself that this was true.

Veronica James sighed and took another sip of her coffee, reveling in the peace of the moment as she soaked in the sight of a pink dawn breaking over the rolling hills of the Columbia Valley. A gentle breeze teased her hair and a small bird trilled a welcome to the day. From the balcony of Gram's apartment, above The Book Nook, it seemed as though she could see forever.

What a lovely way to start the day.

After the last few years, she needed this. She needed this so much.

When her cousins called to say they were worried about Gram and were considering putting her in a nursing home, coming here had seemed the perfect solution. In fact, it was more than a solution for Gram. It was a solution for Veronica, too. Once she'd made the decision to make the move, she'd been suffused with an unfamiliar sense of…peace.

So she'd packed up and left Seattle—where she'd lived since college—and moved to the town she'd considered home during her nomadic childhood. No matter where Dad had been stationed, Veronica had spent all her summers here with Gram. This beautiful spot was the one place in the world where she'd always felt welcome. Safe. At home. Every memory of her childhood summers here was a treasured one. Veronica had loved it here. She'd been her true self here. She'd liked that girl; that girl was afraid of nothing.

Maybe she could find that girl again.

Even though coming back here should have been a no-brainer, Veronica had struggled with the decision. If she was being honest with herself, fear had been the culprit. A deep, dark fear that the ugliness that had shadowed her would follow. That it might infest and taint her most treasured memories.

Or, worse, that she might discover there was no safe place in the world after all. That the sense of belonging and peace she'd experienced in Butterscotch Ridge had been a childish illusion. It was too early to make a decision on any of that. But she'd made it through the last couple of nights without any nightmares. That in itself was a minor miracle.

With a happy sigh, she finished her coffee, picked up her plate and headed down the hall to the kitchen at back of the small apartment. She poked her head in to Gram's bedroom as she passed, just to check on her.

The bed was empty.

A hint of worry trickled through her, so she hurried onward. Gram wasn't in the living room, or in the kitchen. The bathroom was empty, too. Where could she be?

After dropping her dishes in the sink, Veronica pulled a sweater on over her sleeveless shirt to ward off the morning chill—which the sun wouldn't burn off until later—and headed down the front stairs into the bookstore Gram had opened after her retirement.

She stopped short. Her breath caught. Her heart thudded as she took in the ransacked shop. Had they been vandalized? Books had been pulled from the shelves and strewn all about.

"Gram?" she called, trying to control the waver in her voice. "Gram?"

"Here, dear." Gram's soft voice floated from the other side of the jumbled bookstore.

It took Veronica a moment to find her amid the teetering piles of novels, but there she was, peeping over the books with her hair awry, her glasses askew and her eyes alight.

"What on earth did you do?" Last night, they'd finally gotten every book firmly shelved by genre and in alphabetical order by author. Now...well, now there appeared to be no order whatsoever.

Gram shot her a grin. "I'm organizing," she said.

Oh, dear. This kind of impulsive behavior was probably why Max and Gwen had been worried. But really, did it matter? If reorganizing made Gram happy? Hardly anyone came to The Book Nook anymore—probably on account of the fact that Gram didn't like letting go of her favorite books. And they were *all* her favorite books.

"Can I help?" Veronica asked, making her way through the piles.

"Of course," Gram said happily. "You can do those." She pointed to several stacks of romance novels. Gram had always loved romance.

Veronica patted her shawl-covered shoulder. "All right."

"Unless you want to make some molasses cookies?" Gram gave her a sly look. Besides her love of reading, she'd always had a wicked sweet tooth.

Veronica grinned. "Sure. Perhaps I'll make some later."

Gram nodded, delighted at the prospect.

"I think there are still some lemon bars left. Would that do for now?" She'd baked a pan of them yesterday.

"Oh, yes, please."

After a lovely break featuring lemon bars and chamomile tea, and several hours of reorganizing and re-reorganizing novels, the bell on the door rang. Gram didn't even hear it—she was too absorbed in the stacks—but Veronica jumped. Unexpected noises still made her react like that sometimes. She was getting better, but occasionally surprises pierced her newfound calm. It was a process, after all.

She let out a relieved sigh when she recognized a familiar face coming through the door of the shop. Her lips curved upward into a smile, and her pounding heart turned from trepidation to delight.

"Sam!" Veronica headed toward the door, knocking over a stack of historical romances in her rush. Samantha Stirling had been one of her best buddies during those long summers in Butterscotch Ridge. Though they'd seen each other a few days ago, it had been a short visit. Sam had just been showing her new sister-in-law around town so there hadn't been much time to catch up.

Sam greeted her with a bear hug and, without thought, Veronica allowed it. Gosh, it felt nice. The warm, comforting hug of a friend. It had been a while since anyone had hugged her.

"I see you escaped from the ranch," Veronica teased.

Sam Stirling was a bona fide country girl who broke horses and herded cattle and all that stuff that had seemed so romantic and exciting back when they were young. Probably still was. To Sam, at least.

Sam threw back her head and laughed. "I snuck out," she said conspiratorially "Don't tell DJ." DJ was her oldest brother. Now that their grandfather had passed, he was—for all intents and purposes—in charge of the family business. The selfsame ranch where Veronica had spent the summers of her youth.

Because she knew Sam was teasing, Veronica slapped her hand to her chest and said melodramatically, "I swear, I won't say a word." Not that it would matter. She'd never once seen any of the Stirlings lose their temper with Sam. Besides, to be honest, of the four Stirlings, Sam was, by far, the bossiest. She pretty much did what she wanted to do regardless of what DJ, Luke or Mark thought.

And, oh, the thought of *him* pinged at her heart.

Rats. She'd done a pretty good job of not thinking about Mark up until now. Not imagining what their reunion might be like. Whom his wife or girlfriend would be—because, of course, he would be married by now.

Not that it mattered. Mark had been her *friend.* He'd kissed her once, when she was fifteen, that was all. It had been a wonderful kiss and she remembered it fondly.

No, she remembered it with reverence. She'd *clung* to it; that sweet memory had been her salvation at times. Something to latch on to when things got too dark.

But to him? To Mark Stirling? To the cutest boy in town? It had been just a kiss. Certainly not his first, considering how good it had been. He'd probably long ago forgotten that moment in a swirling sea of other memories, other encounters.

She didn't know why that made her feel maudlin, unless it was the backwash of emotion from her angsty teen years. They'd been kids, after all. Aside from that, she wasn't interested in kissing anyone now. Or ever. She'd sworn off men and relationships, and for a damn good reason.

Sam glanced at the empty plates on the table, covered with lemon-bar leavings…not that there were many crumbs left. “I don’t suppose you have any more of that coffee cake from the other day?” She was really good at waggling her eyebrows, and took a moment to show off her skills.

Veronica shook her head to loosen all thoughts of her first, and lost, love. “Um, you mean the coffee cake you and Lizzie devoured the last time you were here?”

“It was damn good. Maybe you can make some more?”

Sam’s praise lit a warm glow within her, and the batted lashes, a smile. The thought of making goodies for Sam, anyone really, somehow wiped away her ennui, the way a baker wiped clean her pastry mat before beginning anew. What a lovely visual.

“How are you doing, Milly?” Sam asked, making her way through the room to give Gram a hug.

“Why does everyone keep asking me that? I’m fine.” And she turned her attention back to her work.

Sam surveyed the deconstructed library and commented, “And look what you’ve done to the place.” Her sarcasm was starchy. As though someone had ironed it.

Astonishingly, Veronica found herself chuckling again. Twice in one day might be a record. “That wasn’t me. Gram is reorganizing.” Though the bookstore looked as though a hurricane had hit, somehow

Gram knew the exact location of each and every volume in the place.

"Is that what the kids are calling it? Reorganizing?"

Sam's dry observation sent a warm reminiscence through Veronica's heart. How many times had she howled with glee at one of Sam's snarky comments?

This place was good for her. She could feel it.

"Well, it keeps her happy," Veronica said, *sotto voce*, even though Gram was hard of hearing.

"You're sweet," Sam said. "Gwen loses her mind when Milly unshelves—"

"That's because Gwen still thinks this bookstore can make it financially." Not that it mattered. When Gram retired from working at Stirling Ranch, she'd bought this property outright. It had a live-in apartment upstairs and lots of shelves from back in the day, when it had been a five-and-dime, before it had been an auto-parts store and a plethora of other things. Gram had long dreamed of owning a bookstore, even though hardly anyone in Butterscotch Ridge read anything other than the *Farmers' Almanac*. Still, she'd filled the shelves with a variety of used books—mostly fiction, but she was fond of encyclopedias and craft workbooks, as well. So what if people rarely came in? All that mattered was that Gram was happy, and there was enough money to pay property taxes. Fortunately, when her husband passed, long before Roni was born, he'd left her a nest egg.

Sam patted Veronica's shoulder. "I'm sure you can find a way to make this place work."

"Not as a bookstore." Not in this town.

"As something." Sam shrugged. "You're clever."

"Am I?" Veronica hadn't felt particularly clever lately. Not since that day in March two years ago. Having your head repeatedly knocked against a tile wall did that. Rattled one's thoughts.

No. No melodrama! She was healing. Maybe she could be clever again someday.

Sam took her hand. "Listen, I didn't come over here to discuss business plans. I'm on my way to the B&G for lunch and I've come to kidnap you."

Oh. Crowds. Something cold whispered across her nape. She shivered.

Veronica glanced at Gram, who'd found a book that—apparently—needed immediate rereading, and was curled up on the couch, among tilting heaps of other tomes. "I should stay with Gram."

"I'm not an invalid," Gram barked without looking up. "No matter what Gwen seems to think."

Sam immediately grasped at that straw. Urging Veronica into mischief had always been one of her stellar traits when they were kids. "Oh, come on. We need to catch up."

"But Gram—" Her hesitation wasn't about Gram. Not really. It was probably wrong to use her as an excuse, but the thought of being around that many people, strangers, unable to see all angles… It gave her the willies.

"Heck. She can come along. Hey, Milly," Sam called. "How about some lunch?"

Gram waved a dismissive hand and barely lifted her head as she called back, "Can't. Reading."

To which Sam responded with a broad, triumphant grin. "Come on, buttercup. Let's get a bite together."

Gram lifted her head. "Go. I promise I won't burn the place down."

Sam shrugged and offered a wicked grin. "And if she does, we're just down the street."

Veronica sighed, but she allowed Sam to hook arms and pull her onto the street and into the sunshine, which was far too bright. "Wait," she said, and then flipped the Open sign to Closed and pulled the door shut, on the off chance someone might be inclined to come in, with a sudden desire for literature, and disturb Gram's peace.

"Look at you. Still a *good girl*," Sam said as they walked down the broad Main Street sidewalk to the only restaurant in town, which was, conveniently, just down the street. Everything in Butterscotch Ridge was conveniently just down the street. Trouble was, there wasn't much. A restaurant, a liquor store, a sadly deficient grocery store… Oh, there was a gas station, and a park and a church and all the things a small town needed. What it lacked was options.

Anyone who wanted anything out of the ordinary had to go to the Tri-Cities—Kennewick, Pasco and Richland—nearly an hour away or Spokane, which was two hours.

Veronica toyed with the buttons on her sweater. It was a little too warm to be wearing a sweater, but she was used to it. "You say that like being a *good girl* is a bad thing."

"The patriarchy wants us to be good girls, remember? Ergo, it is incumbent on us to misbehave and have a roaring good time as often as possible." This, Sam Stirling said with the blasé conviction of a woman who'd never truly been broken.

Of course, it was wrong to make such assumptions about people. Veronica had learned that so well during her marriage and the ensuing months of therapy, but still...she could see it in Sam. That lightness of spirit, a purity of self-acceptance, an easiness of being. It was clear she'd never been taken apart like a jigsaw puzzle and put back wrong. All *her* pieces were still in place. *She* wasn't afraid of anything.

Though Veronica smiled and murmured something that sounded like accord, she knew better than to let herself slip into such a mindset again. It was too dangerous to give in to the longing to let herself go and live without fear. How on earth did a person do that?

Even though Veronica had made a sacred vow not to be ruled by fear, she wasn't stupid. A woman had to protect herself in this world. A woman had to be careful.

"Here we are," Sam said as she pushed open the double doors of the Butterscotch Ridge Bar & Grill, which everyone called the B&G for short. "Chase McGruder owns it now. Do you remember him?"

Veronica shook her head, but it didn't matter. Sam rattled on. "He bought the restaurant, then the bar next door, knocked out the wall, and voilà." She gestured, like Vanna White, to the bright and airy establishment, featuring a restaurant on the left side and a bar on the right. "You want a booth or a table?"

"A booth, please." A table was too exposed. "It smells so good in here." A mélange of scents wafted by, dominated, in good part, by the heavenly aroma of frying potatoes. It was, pretty much, a burger joint, after all.

"You're probably hungry," Sam said. This observation was followed by a quick once-over. "You look like you could eat."

Veronica tried not to wince. Yes. She was skinnier than she should be. That's what happened when a person didn't have an appetite. Some days it was a challenge to make sure she ate three meals. Cooking for Gram helped a little. Baking helped a lot.

"What's good?" Veronica asked as she reviewed the menu.

Sam grinned. "Don't ask me. I'll eat anything." She set herself to the task of reading the menu, making soft *mmm*s every now and again. And then… "Ooh, *bacon*."

Being with her old friend felt so familiar, it made Veronica smile. She didn't even have to try.

By the time the waitress, a pretty brunette with a long ponytail named Crystal, came to their table, Veronica had settled on a salad, because she really wasn't hungry after that lemon bar.

Sam ordered a cheeseburger with a side of onion rings for the table.

Crystal left to go place their order and Veronica turned to Sam. "So," she said. "How's your family?"

"Good," Sam said. "Pretty much the same. Except Luke."

"Luke?" He was the youngest of the Stirling boys, but still a little older than Sam. "What happened to him?"

"Ah, well, he went and joined the Marines. He was in Afghanistan and…" Sam shook her head. "There was an explosion. An IED. Luke survived, but he was badly hurt. He spent months in physical therapy, learning to walk again." Her face went pink. "Oh. Don't tell anyone that. Luke swore me to secrecy. Just like him, you know. He doesn't want anyone to know how rough it really was. He hates sympathy. He equates it with pity."

"Of course not." Veronica shook her head, but her mind was reeling.

She had also spent months in physical therapy

learning to walk again. To feel like herself again. The hardest part had been learning to do makeup—without looking like a child playing with her mommy's lipstick—due to the tremor caused by damage to the tendons in her left wrist. She was recovering, but the process was both a physical and an emotional one. Thankfully, it hadn't kept her from the baking she so loved—as long as she wore the wrist brace her doctor had recommended, she could go on with her activities in the kitchen.

"I-I'd like to see him again," she said, easing back to give Crystal room to deliver their drinks.

Sam grinned. "You will. It's a small town. And he lives just around the corner."

Veronica gaped at her. "He doesn't live at the ranch?"

"That's a tender point, as I am sure you can imagine. For some reason, he refuses to live in *the old man's* house. They never got along, you see."

"But your grandfather's dead, isn't he? Gram told me he died."

"Doesn't matter to Luke."

Veronica sat back and thought about her experiences, and she had to admit, she understood why Luke might want to isolate himself. "He probably just wants his privacy."

"Privacy, schmivacy. Hell, when Mark decided he wanted his privacy, he at least had the good sense to move into one of the cabins on the ranch."

At the sound of his name, Veronica's pulse spiked. "He, ah, moved out of the house?"

Sam looked a little sheepish. "Well, we might have told him to move out. His dogs were annoying our grandmother."

"His…dogs?"

"Ugh. Don't ask." She took a slug of her iced tea. "Oh, I told him you were in town. He seemed excited." Sam offered a conspiratorial wink.

Why did her breath catch at that? Why did her hopes rise?

There was no reason for hope. No need for it. She'd made her choice. She'd come here to heal. To find herself again. The last thing she wanted or needed in her life was another man.

The last one had nearly killed her.

Chapter Two

Mark picked up his pace as he rounded the corner from the parking lot to the B&G. He knew better than to be late for a lunch with Sam, but he'd been in the middle of the back forty repairing a fence and he'd lost track of time. Besides, whatever she wanted to talk about couldn't be more important than repairing the fence before they moved the herd, could it?

Something caught his eye in the window—something red—and he stopped short. His heart gave a hard *ker-thump*; something tingled in his solar plexus. It took his brain a second to catch up and it hit him like an anvil.

Roni. It was *Roni.*

Lord, she was pretty. No. She'd been pretty as a kid; she'd blossomed into beautiful. Her skin was a creamy hue, and her smile dazzled, even through the window of the B&G. Her hair was a deeper shade of red now, and pulled up into a casual bun with escaping strands that wisped around her face. The look definitely suited her. He knew he needed to stop staring, but it took effort.

Damn it. Sam should have given him a heads-up. It would have been nice to have been prepared for this. He was dressed in work clothes. He hadn't taken a shower. He probably smelled like…cow manure or something. He should turn around, get into his car and go back to the ranch. Call Sam and tell her he'd been delayed. Or the heifer had gone into labor. Or the barn had burned down. Anything to avoid meeting Roni again in this cowboy-ugly condition. First impressions were important. This was almost like a first impression, wasn't it? After thirteen years?

If she saw him like this, she'd—

Damn it. Just then Sam spotted him and jerked her head, gesturing to him as if to say "get in here, doofus."

Well, hell. There was nothing for it. He sucked in a deep breath, tucked in his shirttails, raked back his hair and pushed through the door. As he neared the table, his pulse sped up. He'd imagined how this reunion would go since Sam mentioned Roni was in town. But now that it was happening, his mind went utterly blank. The closer he got, the more stunning she seemed.

Even though it had darkened a bit over the years, her hair still highlighted her green-and-amber eyes. The freckles still danced over her nose and her bow-shaped lips set his imagination on fire.

What would he say to her? What could they talk about? What—

The awkwardness melted in the face of another emotion swelling from the well of his being. What if her husband was here, too? How would *that* conversation go? The thought made him feel a little ill.

"Well, hey there," Sam said, lifting her glass as he came up to them. "Look what the cat dragged in."

"You asked me to have lunch today," he reminded her.

"Roni, you remember Mark, don't you?"

Roni's striking eyes met his. They were distressingly blank as she gave her head a little shake. "Um. No. You have a brother named Mark?" she asked Sam.

His heart plummeted. It had never occurred to him that she might not remember him. After all they'd shared? That meant she didn't remember the kiss, either, didn't it? That kiss that he'd held so close to his—

And then he saw it, the sparkle in her eye. The slight quirk of her lips. Indeed, she slid out of the booth and faced him. Laughing.

"Of course I remember you, goofball!" she said, before she bounced her fist off his shoulder.

Without a thought, he gathered her into a hug. She seemed to stiffen at first, as though he'd surprised her, but then, with a sigh, she relaxed into his embrace.

She smelled...divine, fresh, like lemons. Her body

was warm and soft in his arms. A tingle shot up his spine.

He pulled back, waggling a finger. "Never do that again," he said in a gruff voice.

She threw back her head and laughed. "Did you really think I forgot you? How on earth could that ever happen?"

He shrugged. "Well, it's been a long time."

"Sit," Sam commanded, stolidly not making room for him, then waving at the banquette as Roni slid in and scooted over.

Mark slipped in; the space where she'd been was warm. He turned his attention to Roni, taking her in from a closer vantage point. Yup. Still freckled. Still clear-eyed. And, damn, she was all grown up. He offered her a sincere smile. "It's so great to see you again," he said.

Her lips quirked up. "You, too." She shifted sideways in the booth so she could face him better.

"So," he said in the face of her expectant expression. "Thirteen years. Wow." *Jeez, Mark. Way to make sparkling conversation.* "What, ah, what have you been up to?"

For some reason, she paled a bit and glanced away. But then she flashed a brilliant smile, yet somehow, it was a shadow of her former smile. This one didn't seem to reach her eyes. "Not much. How about you?"

"Ah, you know. This and that." *Well, appar-*

ently neither of us are good at this. The thought was somehow comforting to him. But it didn't erase the awkwardness that had settled between them. He didn't like the feeling.

"Mark has a new hobby," Sam offered, but not before she snagged one of the onion rings Crystal dropped off.

Roni waited until after Crystal had taken Mark's order before she asked, "And what's your new hobby?"

Sam answered before he could. "He adopts stray dogs."

"I don't *adopt* them," he clarified. "I *foster* them. And it's not a *hobby*. It's a calling. I work with an organization that places the pets no one else wants."

"He has a herd of them," Sam interjected.

"I think the proper term is *pack*," Mark said. "You know. A herd of cattle, a pack of dogs, a bristle of sisters—"

Sam made a face. "That's not a thing. Anyway—" She turned back to Roni. "I'm convinced he's using them as a surrogate for children, since he can't seem to land a female of childbearing age."

Mark glowered at Sam. "Maybe they're like kids to me. Did you ever think of that?"

Sam tsked. "That's not sad at all."

Mark blew out a breath and turned to Roni, who, it appeared, was enjoying this banter at his expense. "Don't listen to her. My dogs are awesome." He narrowed his gaze. "By the way… We're always looking for good homes for our fur babies. Hint, hint."

"Gadzooks," Sam interrupted. "I shouldn't have mentioned it. Forget I said anything about dogs," she said in a credible Jedi-Master cant.

It didn't work. It never did.

"Do you like Chihuahuas?" Mark asked Roni, mostly to annoy Sam.

"To be honest," she said, though he could tell she was teasing from the smile she couldn't hide, "I believe that if it fits in one's purse, it is not a dog."

"It's not a dog if it can't knock you down," Sam said and they all laughed.

"Are you crying?" Sam asked when Roni dabbed at her eyes with her napkin.

She sighed. "I just forgot how much fun you guys are."

"Yup, that's us." Sam grinned. "We're a barrel of laughs."

And then, apropos of nothing—other than wanting Roni's attention back on him—Mark blurted the thought that had been buzzing in his mind like a hungry mosquito. "I heard you got married."

She went still and paled.

Oh, crap. Maybe he shouldn't have blurted *that* question.

Roni drew in a breath; she toyed with the buttons of her sweater. "That was a long time ago," she said softly. "I'm divorced now."

Through his chagrin, exhilaration rose.

Sam grunted around an onion ring. "Good for you."

Roni glanced at Mark from beneath her lashes. "Are, ah, any of you married?"

She wanted to know if he was available. He couldn't hold back his grin. "Free as a bird."

They all leaned back to give Crystal room to deliver their plates. Both he and Sam had ordered Chase's bacon jam cheeseburgers, while Roni had ordered a salad.

Sam took a big bite of her burger, and Mark followed suit. They moaned in concert.

"Good?" Roni asked over her salad.

"Chase makes a killer bacon jam," Sam said through a mouthful.

"Bacon jam?" Roni's eyebrows came together.

There was no earthly way to explain bacon jam, so Mark held his dripping burger out to her. "There. Taste."

You would have thought he'd offered her raw mountain oysters the way she reared back.

"Go on," he urged. "It's really good."

Roni gave him the side-eye and then reached out and took Mark's burger. Their fingers touched, just barely, but it sent a bolt through him…and through her, if her widening eyes were any measure. She delicately nibbled from the side of the burger he'd not touched.

"So good, isn't it? Go on, take as much as you want," Mark said.

Roni sucked in a breath and tried another bite. This time she got more than bun. "Oh, my God," she said, closing her eyes, obviously glorying in the flavors of grilled meat, toasted bread and that incredible bacon jam. "That is *so* tasty."

"We told you so..." Sam tucked in to her own burger again, not offering anyone a bite, Mark noticed. But he wasn't surprised. She *had* grown up with a houseful of hungry men, after all.

"We do have some exciting news to report," Mark said. Again. With the blurting. It was worth it when Roni turned her attention away from his burger and fixed it on him. "We have a new brother." It was the biggest piece of news that had hit BR in decades.

"She already knows about Danny," Sam said, successfully dampening his enthusiasm.

"I do?" Roni's brow rumpled.

"Remember when I introduced you to Lizzie?"

"Sure."

"Well, she's Danny's wife."

"Danny's our new brother. He's from Vegas," Mark added.

"That is fascinating," Roni said, pretending to be utterly entranced as she rearranged her salad. Mark noticed she wasn't really eating it, and wondered why. But he kept quiet. "How did you find him?"

Sam stole a french fry from Mark's plate and

slathered it in ketchup. "When Granddad died, Danny was named in the will."

"We had no idea he even existed," Mark added.

"Well, *we* did once we clapped eyes on him." Sam leaned in and stole another of Mark's fries. "He looks just like Dad."

Roni's eyes widened. "That's amazing."

Mark nodded. "It was pretty cool."

She gave a soft sigh. "I would have loved to have had a sibling growing up." He knew she was an Army brat who'd grown up all over the world. He couldn't imagine how lonely that must have been as an only child.

"Trust me," Sam said. "Siblings are a pain in the ass. Especially brothers."

"Danny's a great guy. You'll like him," Mark said, on his way to inviting her over for Sunday supper.

Before he could, Sam scuttled his intent once again. "We're having a family supper on Sunday afternoon. Why don't you come and meet him?" she asked.

Roni's eyes lit up, but then her expression fell. "I couldn't. I have to stay with Gram."

"Seriously?" Sam rolled her eyes. "Bring her along."

"Really? You wouldn't mind?"

"Why would we mind?"

"We love Milly," Mark added. Hell, she'd been

like a mother to them for years. Especially after their own mother died.

Sam, like a dog with a bone, continued. "It'll do her good to get out. And it would be great for Grandma, too. Everyone needs friends their own age."

"You should bring her," he said, because he really wanted Roni to come.

Sam nodded. "Show up around noon." And, at Roni's surprise, she chuckled. "We start early."

"It's a family tradition," Mark added, feeling obliged to explain. "We're all so busy, it's a chance to check in with each other."

She shook her head. "I wouldn't want to intrude."

"You're not intruding," Mark said, meeting her gaze. "We'd love the company. Honestly."

Sam pulled out her phone and grimaced. "Damn it. I need to get back to the ranch. You two stay. Chat. Mark, get the bill, will you." It was not a question. Normally he'd squawk at being invited to lunch and left with the bill, but he really wanted to spend more time talking to Roni. Also, he would normally ask his sister what was up at the ranch that might drag her away from lunch, since the whole family was really serious about their food, but frankly, he didn't care. He really didn't want her to stay.

"Bye."

"I guess I'll see you on Sunday, then," Roni said, waving goodbye. Sam wrapped up what was left of her burger—the onion rings were long gone—and left, looking pleased with herself. Mark figured she was, since she'd engineered this reunion. For now, he had Roni alone.

Trouble was… Well, they both had trouble thinking of something to say. Mark madly searched his brain for topics, but nothing came up. It was like that irritating spinning circle on his computer when it was caught in a time loop. Thank God she stepped into the awkwardness first.

"It's so strange seeing you all grown up," she said. "Making the connection to the boy I knew."

He nodded. "I know what you mean. We're different people, but we're not."

"Your face is the same," she offered cheerfully. "Those dimples when you smile. But…"

"But what?" he asked in a teasing tone.

A flush ran up her cheeks. "Well, your body is…"

Is…what? *What?*

"You've certainly filled out." She gestured at his T-shirt-clad chest. He tried not to flex, but it was hard. She'd been his childhood confidante, but she was still an attractive woman.

He forced a friendly smile instead. "That's working on a ranch for you."

"Slinging hay bales, punching cows and all that?"

"Right."

"And what do you do when you're not ranching? Other than fostering dogs?"

"Oh, the dogs don't take much time. Well, maybe they do, but I enjoy taking care of them, so it doesn't feel that way." She continued looking at him expectantly. What more did she want to hear? He hadn't done anything worth that kind of expectation. Not like his brother DJ, who managed the business of the ranch now that Granddad was gone, or Luke, who'd joined the Marines and done two tours in Afghanistan. And Sam was a three-time winner of the annual county calf-roping contest. What had *he* really done with his life? "I'm a volunteer firefighter."

To his relief, this impressed her. Her eyes widened. "You fight fires?"

He nodded, then shrugged. "It's mostly trainings."

"What does firefighter training look like?"

His chuckle escaped on its own. "Probably not what you're visualizing. It's a bunch of local businessmen and ranchers starting fires and then putting them out in the middle of nowhere. Sometimes we have special sessions on electrical fires and chemical fires because you have to handle those differently. We also have CPR refreshers..." Was he as boring as he sounded to himself? Why was he still talking? Why was she still listening? But she was.

"That sounds very exciting."

"Yeah. It gets me off the ranch."

Her smile became mischievous. "And if I'm remembering correctly, you always were a little pyromaniac."

Heat crawled up his cheeks. Oh, God. She remembered that. "Yeah. We've replaced that shed."

"Good to know."

Somehow, the reference to his aborted career as an arsonist when he was five launched them into a raucous game of Remember When. He hadn't realized how many memories he had of her from those days, but bringing them up now made him remember even more.

Running through the sprinklers in their bathing suits.

Climbing the cherry trees to claim their harvest before the birds got them all.

Eating Popsicles until their tongues turned blue.

Oh, his siblings had been with them much of the time, but in his mind, these were memories of Roni.

And then when they got older, he'd started seeing her as something more than a coltish playmate with freckles on her nose. He didn't know why he'd kissed her that day. She'd just looked so...pretty with the sun shimmering through the leaves of the apple tree. Something about her had suddenly seemed... different. It might have become something—*they* might have become something—if she'd come back the next summer...but she hadn't.

They lingered longer over lunch than they probably should have, but Mark was loath to end this reunion. Amazing how the awkwardness of those thirteen years apart seemed to evaporate. He didn't even realize the time until DJ texted him to ask where the hell he was.

He sighed heavily and shoved his cell back into his pocket. "Well, I should probably get back. I've really enjoyed seeing you again."

"Oh, me, too. This has been lovely."

And then, he blurted, "Would you like to have dinner with me sometime? You know, so we can really catch up?"

"Oh, Mark." She set her hand on his. It was warm. Soft. "I would love that."

"Unfortunately, this is the only place in town." He winked.

She chuckled. "It's not so bad."

"Would tonight work?" Hopefully his tone wasn't too eager.

Her smile dimmed. So did his mood. "I need some time to get one of my cousins to stay with Gram. Tomorrow, maybe?"

"Sure. Can I pick you up at six?"

She beamed at him. "Make it seven."

He grinned because everything had worked out so perfectly.

It could not have gone better.

After lunch, Veronica found herself infused with a marvelous energy and sense of well-being—the kind she hadn't felt for, well, years, really. Chatting with Sam and Mark had seemed to renew her spirit. The conversation had been funny and enlightening and Mark's body next to hers had been so warm—

She cut that thought right off.

Yes. He was probably the most attractive man she'd ever seen, with that perfectly sculpted face, a scruffy beard and muscles…

Oh, heavens. His forearms had been thick and veined and his T-shirt had been laminated to his cut abs.

He'd had that kind of scent that drove women crazy—a mix of manly musk and sweat from plain old hard work. Every time he moved, she'd gotten a whiff of it.

If she'd been in the market for a hunk…

But she wasn't.

She was, however, in the market for a friend, and he fit the bill perfectly.

Now that he was back in her life, it felt as though everything was finally back on track. She didn't bother to explore that revelation too closely, she just enjoyed the feeling; it had been so long in coming.

Gram had finished reshelving and had gone down for a nap when she got home so Roni, still feeling high on life, headed for the kitchen.

Of all the things she used to love, baking was at the top of the list. And it was a long list. Her job teaching children, listening to music, laughing…

chocolate. Who would ever believe a person could fall out of love with chocolate? Unthinkable! But it had happened.

For Veronica, chocolate had been the canary in the coal mine. Her disinclination to imbibe—because of *disinterest*—had been the red flag she'd finally seen. By then, it had been too late.

The depression had snuck up on her, like a marauder from the shadows. She hadn't even realized she was depressed, not until the *incident* had forced her to acknowledge her PTSD.

Funny, how hard depression was to overcome. Roni and her therapist—the amazing Gretchen—had worked out a treatment plan that included trying various medications until they found the right combination, along with trying acupuncture, yoga, self-defense courses and more. Some things helped for a while, but then, the darkness would return, sometimes worse than ever. But Veronica refused to let it own her, and had fought with every tool at her disposal to maintain the equilibrium she'd struggled to rebuild.

There had been a lot of other little passages. Filing for divorce, filing a restraining order in case Anthony got out of jail, changing her surname from Randall back to James. Tiny steps for sure, but each one led her back to herself.

This was *her* life, by God. She would not let anything or anyone control her.

After living so long under that cloud, it was refreshing and exhilarating to have something to look forward to.

She wondered how much of this giddy feeling had to do with her reunion with Mark. That hug, that unexpected, all-encompassing acceptance, had shifted something in her. Made her feel...protected, free, released by the darkness. Or some of it, anyway.

Recovery was a journey of tiny steps, Gretchen had told her, but, with diligence, there was a way out. Roni hadn't believed her. Not really. But now, she was starting to see it. Starting to glimpse a future where happiness could blossom again.

She strapped on her wrist brace and turned to the kitchen to express her joy. Just as she used to do when she was happy—a long time ago.

By dinnertime, she realized she might have gone a little overboard, but as she looked around the crowded countertops—at several batches of cookies, a cake and a pan of seductive dark-chocolate brownies—she didn't feel a hint of guilt. Yes. It was a lot. Way more than she and Gram could ever eat, but it was beautiful. And she felt wonderful. As though she'd done something to reward herself for putting herself out there today. For leaving this structure. For being social.

Granted, this much sugar was hardly healthy, but who was she to split hairs?

It was a good thing that she and Gram were going to the ranch on Sunday. The thought of an appreciative crowd of Stirlings devouring her baking lightened her mood even more, and she chuckled at the visual in her mind.

"What's so funny?" Gram asked as she shuffled into the room in her pajamas and slippers even though it was hours away from bedtime. Unsure if this was something new, or just new normal, Veronica made a mental note to quiz Gwen about Gram's recent behavior changes.

"I'm just happy," Veronica said, giving her a kiss on the cheek. "Here, have a cookie."

Gram wrinkled her nose. "Is it molasses?"

"Of course."

She came over to survey the platter. Sniffed...and smiled. "Mmm," she said, taking two. "I like them when they're chewy."

Veronica poured two glasses of milk and joined her at the table. They sat and munched and totally ignored the fact that they should be having something sensible for dinner.

As they sat in silence—because Gram often went silent nowadays—Veronica thought about her day. Lunch with Sam had been great, for sure. Reuniting with her was proving to be a much-needed respite from her loneliness. But, if she was being honest, it had been Mark's presence that had truly delighted her.

That, and the fact that they'd seemed to just step back into that easy friendship they'd once shared. Easy, warm…and safe. Yes. There was that about him.

In all their summers together, he'd saved her from childhood perils—like the time he'd led her to the pond to outrun the hornets when she'd kicked over a nest. The time he'd rescued her when she'd climbed too high in the old oak tree. The time he'd untangled her hair when she'd gotten it caught in a nail in the barn. Silly things, really, but they mattered. They left an impression of the kind of kid he was.

The kind of man she suspected he'd grown up to be.

Oh, how often in Seattle she'd wished for just one friend like Mark. Just one person who cared for her and liked her and laughed at her jokes. One person she could trust, who would make her feel like…herself.

Anthony hadn't been any of those things. Not even in the beginning, she now realized.

Anthony had—

No. She shook her head. She was not going to think about him. About that.

Gretchen always said it took discipline to focus on the positive. And sometimes, it took determination, too. Veronica was *determined* she was not going to let Anthony eclipse this happiness.

Better to focus on tomorrow's dinner with Mark.

And, oh, now that she thought about it, she remembered she needed to call her cousins to see if one of them could stay with Gram while she went out. It would be hard to relax and really enjoy catching up with Mark if she didn't make those arrangements.

She was just reaching for her cell phone when someone knocked on the door.

"Come in," Gram called. She didn't even ask who it was first. Veronica sighed. Maybe she did need a sitter.

Her cousin Gwen pushed through the door with her twin toddlers, Charlie and Tiffany, in tow. "Hey, guys," she called.

"Oooh!" Veronica zeroed in on Tiff, who was dressed in a princess dress with a tiara and wand and everything. "Look who's here." When she opened her arms, Tiffy threw herself into a sticky hug. Veronica hugged her back. Clung, a little, perhaps, because Tiffany was soft and smelled of powder and strawberries. She was full of hope and possibilities.

Kids this age had always been irresistible to her.

"Look," Tiffy said, thrusting an amorphous pink-and-purple blob of sugar in Veronica's face.

"Wow," she said, but only because it seemed expected.

And then, when Tiffy demanded, *"Taste!"* she pretended to do so and then dissolved into rapturous sounds, which made the little one giggle. But, seriously, the candy—whatever it was—was covered with dirt and a little bit of hair. So yeah. No thanks.

When Tiffy lost interest in her and bolted for Gram, Veronica took Charlie from Gwen's arms and gave him a cuddle. He was the quieter of the two, and he stared at her with big brown eyes as he sucked on two fingers.

"I hope you don't mind us coming by," Gwen said.

"Not at all. It's great to see you!"

"We were in the neighborhood and I had some leftover casserole I wanted to bring by for Gram. Last time I made it she really liked it. You know how hard it is to get her to eat sometimes." She paused and glanced at the crumbs on the plates, and then, at the array of carbohydrates dominating the countertops. She chuckled. "Well, I guess you figured out Gram has a sweet tooth."

"These are for Sunday," Veronica responded, almost defensively, though she didn't need to justify her every move, not anymore. But old habits were hard to break. She forced a smile. "Gram and I are going over to the Stirlings for supper and I thought I'd bring some desserts."

Gwen arched an eyebrow. "Some? You could stock a bakery with all this stuff."

All right. Maybe it was a bit…excessive. "Do you want to take some home?"

Gwen shook her head. "I'd love to, but I'm on a diet and sugar just hops the kids up."

Veronica glanced at Tiffy, who was dancing around the kitchen singing about a baby shark at the top of her lungs, but she refrained from commenting on purple-and-pink globs of sugar. She was hardly the one to give parenting advice.

Gwen dug into her enormous Mom bag and pulled out a Tupperware container. "It's salmon loaf," she said as she handed it over.

"Oh, nummy."

"Just nuke it for a few minutes. Not too hot, though. Gram forgets to check the temperature and last time she burned her mouth."

"Right. Thanks." Veronica let Charlie down and put the meal into the fridge. "Oh, while you're here, I wanted to ask if there's any way you can stay with Gram tomorrow night."

"Don't need a sitter." This from Gram.

Gwen, who had helped herself to a cookie, sat at the table with a thud. "What's tomorrow night? Umm." She looked at Veronica in ecstasy, lips covered in crumbs. "This is *good*."

"Thanks. Yeah, well, I have dinner plans and I don't want to leave her alone." She lowered her voice, because Gram was listening. "You know. It's only the B&G, but I worry."

"Dinner plans?" Gwen's brow soared skyward. "With whom?"

A trickle of discomfort slid through her. She didn't want to talk about Mark with Gwen, but she wasn't sure why. However, her cousin was waiting, staring at her like a curious owl, so she sucked in a deep breath and said, "Mark Stirling," in the most nonchalant tone she could muster.

Silence hummed. When she glanced at Gwen, it was to find her staring, mouth agape.

"What?" she asked.

"You have a dinner *date* with Mark Stirling?"

Heat crawled up Veronica's cheeks. "It's not a date. We're just going to catch up. You know. It's been thirteen years."

Gwen snorted. "Mark Stirling does not take women out to *catch up*."

"What do you mean?"

"Look, Veronica, you've been away a long time. The last time you saw him you were, what, twelve?"

"Fifteen." He'd been sixteen.

"Well, Mark Stirling isn't exactly a boy anymore." Oh, no. He was clearly a *man*.

"What are you trying to say?"

"He's the biggest playboy in Butterscotch Ridge."

"He is not." What a terrible thing to say. He was the sweetest guy she'd ever met.

"He eats virgins for lunch."

"Gosh, I had lunch with him today and all he had was a burger."

Gwen's eyes widened. "You had lunch with him

today and you're going to dinner tomorrow? What are you thinking?"

"Technically I had lunch with Sam. Mark showed up. And he had a burger."

"Maybe there weren't any virgins on the menu? Look, Veronica, I just don't think you understand what you're getting yourself into. The man will break your heart and toss you aside. It's in his DNA."

Veronica drew in a deep breath. She had no intention of launching herself into a romance of any kind. That Gwen thought so poorly of Mark bothered her. She ignored the fact that the thought of him romancing the entire county made her belly ache. "It hardly matters. It's not a date. We're just catching up."

"Mmm-hmm." Gwen nodded. "You just keep telling yourself that. But you can bet your brownies, *he* thinks this is a date."

"I don't want to bet my brownies," she grumbled. "Look, can you do it, or not?"

"Of course I can do it. Roger can watch the kids for once." She glanced over at Charlie, who was methodically pulling items out of the trash and arranging them on the floor. Meanwhile, Tiffy was crawling around on her hands and knees and barking like a dog. "In fact, I'll probably enjoy the peace and quiet for an evening. Just remember what I said, though, and watch your step with Mark."

"All right," Veronica said, just to end the conversation.

But it was a ridiculous thought. She and Mark were meeting for dinner. A friendly get-together. That was all. It wasn't a date. Surely he knew that.

Didn't he?

Chapter Three

Mark was surprised to find that he was actually nervous about his date with Roni—more than he should have been. After all, they hadn't really talked for thirteen years—they didn't really know each other as adults.

Seven in the evening was actually great timing for a date. The dinner rush was over and the wild antics on the bar side of the establishment wouldn't yet be in full swing. It wouldn't be as quiet, or romantic, as he might wish, but unless he took her to a restaurant in the Tri-Cities—or to his place—there really were no other options.

As eager as he was, he ended up being five minutes late for their date. A tire on his truck had picked up a nail. It took forever to find Sam and ask to borrow her car—DJ's was in the shop and the tractor was just a no-go for a first date, wasn't it? It was frustrating as hell, but by the time he got into town, he had reclaimed his good humor. And why not? He was going on a date with Veronica James. His sixteen-year-old self was fist-pumping with excitement.

After he parked behind the bookstore and levered out of Sam's tiny coupe, he ran a hand through his hair, grabbed the flowers he'd picked up at the grocery store and bounded up the stairs at the back of the building that led to the apartment where Roni and her grandmother lived.

His heart thudded as he knocked. He ran a finger around the neck of his dress shirt, wondering if he should have added a suit jacket and a tie. But, heck, this was Butterscotch Ridge. People might think he was heading for a funeral if he wore something like that. Besides, the shirt was tight enough without the tie. He knocked again and shuffled his feet a bit as he waited for an answer.

He smiled when the door opened…except it wasn't Roni. It was Gwen. *Yikes.* His smile faltered. The hand holding the flowers drooped.

"Hello, Mark," she said dryly. Yeah. There'd never been much love lost between them. Not since high school. She still needled him every time they met.

"Hey, Gwen," he said brightly. "I'm here for Roni."

"Yeah, I know." She turned around and headed back into the apartment without so much as a *come on in.*

He followed her into the small, homey kitchen and looked around. It was a little outdated, but warm. And it smelled fantastic. It didn't take him long to identify why. A couple of pies sat cooling on the counter. Apple, if he didn't miss his guess.

"She's almost ready." Gwen dropped into a chair by the table. She didn't offer him a seat, but he was too nervous to sit, anyway.

"So, how's Roger?" he asked. Not that he really cared, but banal conversation was about all he could manage.

"He's fine. Home with the kids."

"Twins, right?"

She tipped her head and gave him the side-eye, then picked up a pencil and turned back to her crossword puzzle. After a moment she dropped the pencil and glared at him, as though the fact she couldn't solve the puzzle was *his* fault. "If you hurt her, I will eviscerate you," she hissed, apropos of nothing.

Seriously? He'd brought flowers. He'd arrived nearly on time. He'd *shaved*, for pity's sake. "What are you talking about?"

"She's been through a lot, Mark." She said his name as though it tasted bad. "She doesn't need to be toyed with by a...*playboy*."

A playboy? He was about to respond, but just then, Roni emerged from the hallway. And when she smiled at him, he completely forgot whatever it was he was going to say to Gwen.

She wasn't wearing anything fancy—a simple long-sleeved black tunic with black leggings and a silver necklace—but she looked like a million bucks.

"Hi, Mark," she said, giving him a once-over. "Wow. You clean up nice."

He grinned and handed her the flowers. "You look great, too."

"Thank you," she said, but as she turned away to put the flowers in water, he thought he saw her smile dim. Just a little. It was probably his imagination. Maybe he was too sensitive and reading things into her every expression. Hey, maybe she didn't like flowers? Though he'd never met a woman who didn't like flowers. Maybe—

"Are you ready to go?" she asked. When she set the vase of flowers on the table, Gwen pushed it to the far side with one finger.

"You bet." He took Roni's arm and saluted Gwen, who made a face at him because Roni was looking the other way.

"We won't be late," Roni told her cousin as she collected her purse. "And we'll be just down the street if you need anything."

"Don't worry," Gwen said, waving Roni to the door. "Just have fun."

"Thanks," he said, but he could tell his attempt at grace wasn't appreciated. Shrugging it off, he held the door open for Roni. When she passed him as she exited, he got a whiff of her perfume and all thoughts of Gwen, or anyone else, evaporated.

It was a nice night, cool after the warmth of the day. A balmy breeze kicked up her hair, bringing her scent to him once again. As they walked around the corner to Main Street and over to the B&G, they chatted about little things, like the weather, and the fact that she was excited that cherries would soon be in season. It was nice. Sweet. Innocent. He instinctively wanted to take her hand, but curled his fingers into a ball. *Slow*, he reminded himself. *Take it slow.* He had no idea why his heart was pounding like a drum. But then she smiled at him and he knew. Of course he knew.

He opened the door of the restaurant for her, because that's what gentlemen on dates did, and she gave him a cute little curtsy in return.

Chase met them at the door. "Hi, folks," he said. "Table for two?"

Roni smiled. "Yes, please," she said.

"Something in the back?" Chase suggested. "I think it'll be a little quieter back there, once these cowboys get their drink on."

When they nodded, he led them to a table in the corner of the restaurant, far from the bright lights of the bar. It was nice. Almost romantic. Well, as romantic as the B&G got, Mark supposed.

He took his seat across from Roni and they smiled at each other. Crystal appeared with menus and water for them both and then, finally, they were alone. There were a few dinner stragglers at the other tables, but they were all on the other side of the room, and the bar was deserted. It was actually the perfect setting for a first date.

Too bad he was nervous as hell.

Mark folded his hands on the table and gazed at Roni, unsure what to say. He was a little relieved to see that at least she looked a little nervous, too. That was something.

"I'm so glad you could come tonight," he finally said. "I've really been looking forward to this..."

Her smile faded, and his mood deflated, just a little. Then she leaned in, set her hands on his and said the worst possible thing a woman could say to a guy on the first date.

"Mark, I need to tell you something."

Yikes. That sounded...ominous. "Um, okay."

But before she could say anything else, Crystal arrived with their drinks and some dinner rolls, which was awkward. When she asked if they were ready to order, they both asked for a few more minutes, since they hadn't even glanced at the menus. She smiled knowingly and said she'd be back in a bit, leaving them to their uncomfortable conversation.

Mark shifted in his seat. "So, this thing you wanted to tell me about. What is it?"

She smiled, but he could see it was half-hearted. "Don't be so gloomy."

"Oh. Am I being gloomy?" He forced a smile.

"I know this is kind of a weird place for this conversation, but… Don't make this more difficult than it has to be, please?"

Well, hell. Whatever she was going to say would not be something he wanted to hear. He knew it to the core of his being. But she clearly needed to get something important off her chest, and he was going to listen and be respectful. No matter what. "Okay. Shoot."

She toyed with the stem of her wineglass for a minute, then gusted a sigh and said, "Mark…I love that we have a chance to reconnect and reestablish our friendship—" *Friendship? Crap.* "—after all these years. But I have to be honest with you."

His jaw tightened. What? Was she still married after all? Did she have a boyfriend? Or a girlfriend? What?

She drew in a deep breath, sat back and then took a sip of her wine. "This isn't easy for me to talk about."

"Okay…"

"I, um… So, I told you that I was married. And that I went through a divorce."

Yes. Yes. He knew.

She picked up a fork and fiddled with it. She stared at it as though it fascinated her. Or, as though she couldn't bear to meet his eye while she said whatever it was she needed to say. "It was…not a happy marriage."

He nodded, still not sure where she was going with this.

She caught and held his gaze. "It was a very… bad marriage."

There was an undertone in her words. As though she was tiptoeing around some dark secret that was too painful to reveal. It made a cold shiver run down his spine, and suddenly, an instinct to protect her rose up within him. But protect her from what? "I… Ah… Okay," he said, a bit uncertainly.

Her smile, the real one, appeared and it made his chest hurt a little. Because suddenly, he had an inkling as to why she was so hesitant to express herself. "Oh, good. So then you understand why I'm not looking for…romance."

Crap. This felt like she was putting him in the friend-zone. She *was* putting him in the friend-zone. Crap.

The fact that she had a damn good reason for putting him in the friend-zone didn't make him feel any better—for himself, and definitely not for her.

Still, he smiled encouragingly.

Relief washed over her face. "Thank God. Gwen was certain you thought…" She sat back and stared at him for a moment, then reached out for him, taking his hand. "Thank you so much for understanding."

"Of course. Sure… Everyone needs time after a bad divorce." That much he did understand.

To his horror, her expression clouded again. She pulled away. Shook her head. "Oh, no. It's not that. This isn't about time at all. I've had time." She let out a bitter laugh; he didn't understand why. There was something here just out of his reach. But he didn't know what, or how to ask for more information in a way that might not cross any lines. It was frustrating. Because, sure, he wanted to understand—but he wanted to help, too, if he could.

"Anthony and I have been divorced for over two years."

Okay. Now he *really* didn't get it. After a minute he sallied forth with a question. "So…?"

She took another drink of her wine. A fortifying gulp. "Mark, I'm not interested in dating. Not at all. Not ever again."

Bitterness rose in his throat. "Never?" He had to wonder what the hell could have happened in her marriage to make her swear off the possibility of love…for good. The prospect haunted him.

"Never." She picked a roll from the basket and absentmindedly shredded it. "See, I made a decision. I decided *I* am enough. I don't need a relationship to define me. A *romantic relationship*, I mean." When he didn't respond, she continued. "I need you to understand where I'm coming from."

He didn't. Not completely. But that didn't matter now. His stupid hopes for dazzling her with his charm most certainly didn't matter now. Something—no, someone—had wounded her. All he wanted was to hold her. To make it better somehow. But he couldn't. Not really.

Right now she needed him. He could be there for her right now. That had to be enough. She'd meant something to him when they'd both been kids. She meant something still. And he would honor that.

"Okay." He took a sip of his wine, then smiled at her. "I'm here for you, Roni. Whatever you need."

Obviously something in his expression or his tone, something unintended, had given him away. "Oh." Tears glimmered in her eyes. "You did think this was a date, didn't you? Oh, I should have known it. Gwen was right."

This information, of course, made him frown. It kind of bugged him that Gwen might be right about something. Anything. But he hated the look on Roni's face even more. The bald fact was…she was different. She was *special.* She'd always been special to him for some reason. He wasn't sure what it was that made her different from all the other women he'd known, but he *knew* she was.

Maybe the fact that her jokes made him laugh, or things were just easy and natural between them. He'd never had any of those things with someone else.

If she wanted friendship, well, he respected her enough to give her what she wanted. They'd been friends as kids, and it had been pretty great; he could try and forget that kiss. They'd practically been children. Or so he tried to convince himself.

If friendship was all she wanted, that would have

to be enough. He couldn't have all of her, but he could have whatever she was willing to offer. And he'd accept, gladly.

"I'm sorry," she said.

Mark nodded and glanced at his glass, remorseful now that it was empty. He could have used another snort. "I'm sorry, too." Sorry. It was a simple word, hardly strong enough to carry the weight of his feelings. "I'm so sorry. For whatever happened that made you feel this way."

Silence surrounded them again. "So you're not disappointed?"

"Crushed." He rolled his eyes. And, yeah, as he always did when he was in an uncomfortable spot, he went straight for humor. "Hell, I had us walking down the aisle with three kids and a dog."

She stared at him and then her lips quirked. "Just one dog?"

He threw back his head and laughed. "Okay, you got me. There might have been more than one dog in my fantasy."

"But, we're still friends, right?" she asked. As though she didn't already know. Which kind of broke his heart.

"Roni, we will always be friends." The words were sharp and hurt in his mouth, but they were true. "And," he added after a moment's thought, "I'm here for you, however you want me. If you ever want to talk, if you need a shoulder to cry on, a brownie taster..."

And, ah, when she grinned, she glowed. “Thank you, Mark. You can’t know how much that means to me.” But the tears in her eyes gave her away.

He squeezed her hand. “Why don’t we order dinner?”

“You bet. I’m starving.”

He nodded and signaled the waitress with a blasé smile on his face, but somewhere, deep down in his soul, he ached for the happy girl he used to know. And he wondered yet again what—and who—had hurt her so badly.

That night, Roni had trouble sleeping. Part of it was lying awake and thinking about how much she’d enjoyed the evening with Mark.

But she also had the dream again. It hit her harder than it should have—that dark cacophony of noise, lights and pain. Screams. She shot up in bed, covered in sweat and panting, filled with an unaccountable dread.

It took her a while to calm. She was here. In her bed at Gram’s. The comforter was familiar and worn. The faint scents of butter and sugar still hung in the air from her baking earlier in the day. She was alone in the room. There was no one in the shadows. Still, it took several minutes for her thudding pulse to slow. Longer for her to stop shaking.

She had to clutch the furniture as she made her way to the bathroom for a drink of water. Catching her reflection in the mirror, she flinched, hating the way she looked. Afraid and hunted. Wounded, as the ugly spiderweb of scars on her bare shoulder and back attested.

He's not here, she wanted to shout to herself, to the world. Of course, she couldn't. It wouldn't do to wake Gram or frighten the neighbors. How long would it be, she wondered, before the memory of him no longer had this hold on her? What would it take?

Well, there was no more sleep coming. That, she knew for certain. Instead, she dressed in the outfit she'd chosen for today's trip to Stirling Ranch and made her way into the kitchen.

There was a lot to look forward to, she reminded herself. She hadn't been to the ranch since…wow. Since she was fifteen. So long ago. She couldn't wait to see it again. Couldn't wait to be together with the entire family again.

Especially Mark.

Although, if she was honest with herself, maybe she was a little nervous, too. Seeing him had reminded her of all those happy times, and the girl she'd once been, but it had also reminded her how easy it could be to let physical attraction overwhelm common sense. His smile had made her heart flutter. His touch had sent her pulse into a tumult. There was no doubt she found him as attractive as she had back then—more, perhaps, because now she knew where such things led. Thank God they had an understanding, that he'd been willing to accept her friendship...and nothing more.

He'd been so understanding when she'd told him about her marriage. Granted, she hadn't gone into detail, but he'd seemed to realize it wasn't your average marital disaster, no simple case of irreconcilable differences. Thank God, he hadn't asked for more information. The last thing she wanted to do was tell anyone about the hell her life had been. It was painful to relive and, worse, embarrassing.

Gretchen had told her not to feel shame that she'd been misled by Anthony's manners and charm, that she'd been sucked into an abusive relationship. That she'd stayed as long as she had. It was one thing to hear a message like that, and quite another to internalize it.

Internalization took time. And practice.

Damn it all, anyway, she'd always been a strong woman. How had she let him do what he did?

Silly question. She knew. In group therapy, she'd listened to other women who'd been in the same boat. Many told the exact same story. It had been a slow descent. A seductive one. She hadn't even realized what was happening until she was in too deep. And by then, he had isolated her. Even if she hadn't been too frightened to reach out for help, there had been no one left to help her, because he'd made sure to cut her friends and what little family she had out of her life.

Not too difficult since Mom had passed from cancer, and her father had been busy with his new family on the other side of the planet. Yeah. She'd been all alone by then. Lost, really. Would things have been different if her parents had been there for her? If she hadn't felt so abandoned and alone?

It hardly mattered, because things hadn't happened that way and she'd seen Anthony as her long-anticipated Mr. Right.

The first time he'd hit her, he'd been so repentant. As if he couldn't believe he was capable of such a thing. He'd sworn it would never happen again.

Of course, it had. Of course, she'd allowed it. She had—

No.

She stopped her thoughts abruptly. No. It was not her fault. She was not the guilty party. She was not the one in prison for assault and battery. She'd done nothing to make him want to hurt her. *He* was the broken one.

She stared at her face in the mirror—surely not to see if the scar on her brow was still visible—then shook her head as she tugged her sweater on over the dress. She owed him nothing. He didn't own any part of her. Not even her regrets.

No more thinking of the past. Today was a new day. The future belonged to her.

* * *

Gram was really excited when she woke up. She'd been looking forward to visiting to the ranch all week. So much so, that she insisted on driving.

"I can drive," Veronica said, juggling the desserts in an attempt to take command of the keys.

Gram tipped back her head and sniffed. "I'm not a child. I don't know why you kids insist on wrapping me in cotton wool."

"But, Gram…"

"I've been driving longer than you've been alive, missy."

"But, Gram…"

She glowered. It was truly intimidating. "It's my car. I'm driving. And that's it."

It was, therefore, a nerve-wracking ride, though Gram did very well, aside from refusing to stop for the sign on Fifth and Main because, clearly, the town council had put it there just to annoy her.

Fortunately, it wasn't a long drive. It wasn't long before they passed under the fire-branded sign that read *Stirling Ranch.* When they crested a hill, and Roni saw the house in the distance, a swell of emotion formed a lump in her throat. She wished she was driving so she could stop the car and just soak in the sight.

After everything she'd been through, this truly felt like a homecoming.

It was a silly feeling, really. But that big old

rambling house meant something important to her, touched something deep inside her. Something that made her heart swell with gratitude and joy. It wasn't her house, and it never would be. But to her, it would always be…home.

As a military kid, her family had moved constantly—from Germany to Taiwan to Oklahoma and on. And on. Nothing in her young life had ever been stable…except summers. Summers at this house. With this family. Every season, they'd welcomed her, the awkward little girl with no place to call her own. They'd let her pretend she had siblings, that she had a *place*. She loved them for it, and always would.

Sam was out front to meet them as they pulled into the large gravel lot between the big house and the cabins to the east of the barn. She gave Veronica a huge hug, only a split second after she was out of the car. And then, before she realized what was happening, she was surrounded.

And, oh, what a wonderful welcome. DJ was there, tall and sober-looking, as he always had been. And Luke, who was as strong and commanding as he'd always been, even though his face was now scarred.

Mark was there, too, of course. He opened Gram's door and helped her out, then put her hand on his arm and escorted her into the house as though she was a royal princess and not a persnickety eighty-year-old with a cane.

"Roni, come meet Danny," Sam said, taking her by the hand, and, of course, she followed. She was dying of curiosity, after all. Danny did not disappoint.

This new brother stood on the porch with Lizzie, whom Veronica had met just recently at the bookstore. He caught her attention, and her breath. Dang, he was handsome. Unlike Mark, whose hair was a sandy, sun-kissed brown, Danny had black hair and brown eyes, but their features were stunningly similar. He had the trademark Stirling dimples. That same dent on his chin.

Between Danny and Lizzie stood a miniature, female version of all of them with a mop of dark curls. Roni's heart twanged at the sight of her. She was so beautiful.

"This is Emma," Sam said proudly. "Our very brave niece."

Emma nodded. "I'm very brave," she said in a blasé tone. Then, she added in a conspiratorial tone, "I'm six."

"Are you?" Veronica asked with a smile. Emma was adorable. Beyond adorable. "Are you in kindergarten?" she asked, because, though she was smaller than most of Veronica's past students, she was the right age.

"I've been homeschooled," Emma said with a wrinkled nose. "Because I was really sick. But now that I'm better, I'll get to go to a real school."

She'd been sick? Hmm. Emma did look a bit fragile, but since this was hardly the time or place for questions, Veronica decided to gloss over that tidbit and keep the conversation positive. "Real school sounds like fun. I used to be a teacher, so let me know if you have any questions."

Emma's eyes widened. "Really?" And she took Roni's hand.

Oh, lord. The gesture was so sweet and trusting, it made Roni want to burst into tears. She held them back, of course, but couldn't help sniffling a little. How she missed teaching. How she missed children.

The whole afternoon was like that, warm and welcoming. One delightful interaction after another. Even Gram and Dorthea, the Stirling matriarch, seemed to hit it off. Sam joked that at least getting old was good for something, because the two hadn't exactly been buddy-buddy in their younger years—Dorthea had been Milly's boss after all. But these opposites attracted now that their hair color matched. They drank tea and ate cakes at the table on the long front porch and chatted incessantly about *old times*, while the *kids* lounged in a loose circle on the swings and rockers, and sipped lemonade and nibbled crudités while they watched Emma make and chase bubbles on the lawn.

Danny and Lizzie sat side by side. His arm was draped lazily over her shoulder and his fingers toyed with her hair as they watched their daughter play. It was clear these two were deeply in love. Roni couldn't help being happy for them. When Lizzie mentioned she was expecting again, that happiness grew. Even if it took a little effort to banish the sprig of jealousy that rose within her.

Roni had loved being pregnant—even though she hadn't been for long. She could still remember the joy, the miracle of having a small human sleeping beneath her heart. How could she feel anything but happiness for Lizzie and Danny? A baby was coming. How miraculous was that?

"Hey." Mark nudged her with an elbow. "Are you all right?"

"Me?" She forced a smile. "I'm great."

"Mmm. You looked sad."

She appreciated that he was speaking softly, so no one else could hear. Then again, with all the crisscrossing conversations, who would? Danny and DJ were trying to outyell each other about some football player, Sam and Lizzie were discussing what foods to eat for healthy gut flora, and Luke—who was mostly silent—grimaced each time they mentioned a vegetable.

"I'm not sad," she said. It was a complete and utter falsehood, but God would probably forgive her. To prove how delighted she was, she showed him her teeth.

He laughed. "Right. Hey. You want to go for a walk to the barn? There's something I want to show you. It might cheer you up."

"I said I'm not sad," she insisted, and he gave her a *look*. The kind of look only a friend who truly and deeply cared would give. It said "you don't need to lie to me." She stared into his eyes, somehow lifted by the fact that she could reveal herself to him, scars and all, and he would still like her. Not that she had the courage to reveal herself to him. Or anyone. It would be unfair to dump her story, her issues, on others. She stood and slipped her arm through his extended elbow and said, as they walked down the stairs to the yard, "Are you going to give me a hint as to what it is?"

He snorted a laugh. "It's no mystery. I want to show you our new arrival."

"New arrival?"

"Mmm-hmm." He leaned in and whispered, "It's a calf."

"Oooh." Pleasure trilled through her as they headed off.

She ducked beneath his arm as he swung open the barn door. That familiar musty scent of hay and animals washed over her, triggering a flood of childhood memories—clambering all over the tractor, hiding up in the hayloft, watching the barn cat have her kittens… There, in the pen on the far side of the yawning expanse, stood a perfectly adorable baby cow.

Mark waved her forward. "As promised."

The baby—she named him Boomer, because

Mark said they didn't name their cows and that didn't seem right—was just precious…and just what she'd needed. Something small and innocent and soft to pet. Mark leaned against the fence and watched her face a little too intently. Then he said, for no reason whatsoever, "Why didn't you ever come back?"

It was so unexpected, this query, and it kicked up far too many unpleasant memories; it took her a moment to sift through them, lock them away again and respond. Still, all she could manage was "What?" Then she asked, "What do you want to know?"

He shrugged. "Why don't you start with when you left here that last summer?"

A laugh bubbled up. She had no idea why. "That's a lot of ground you want to cover."

"I always wondered where you were, what you were doing… Why you never came back. Milly wouldn't talk about it."

She turned to him with an apologetic expression. "I would have loved to come back here, but my parents got a divorce that year. Everything changed."

"I'm sorry."

Her barked laugh was bitter. "Me, too. My dad went to Okinawa for several years, where he met his new wife, by the way—"

"I guess he recovered quickly." She appreciated that Mark's tone was dry.

"Then Mom moved to LA. Because her family was there."

"So you lived in LA? What was that like?"

"I loved LA. I didn't realize it for a while, because I was so unhappy about my parent's divorce. And I'd been raised on military bases. Civilian life can be a huge culture shock. But I really did love living there with Grandma and Grandpa." She sighed. "They've all passed now."

"Your mom, too?"

She glanced away. "Yes."

"I'm sorry." He grimaced. "I keep saying that."

She shrugged. "It is what it is. Dad and Betty live in Germany now. He has a new family."

"Do you ever visit?"

"Not anymore." And, when Mark glanced at her, she said softly, "He has a new family."

"I'm sorry."

She set her palm on Boomer's velvety muzzle and he snorted on her. She laughed and dried her hand on her jeans. "Anyway, after high school, I went to college at the University of Washington—"

"Go Dawgs."

"I got a full-ride scholarship."

"Good for you!"

"And got my degree in education."

"Wow."

She glanced at him and leaned on the fence, as he was, staring at her.

He smiled. "Your face just lit up like a beacon."

"Well, I loved it."

He plucked a sprig of straw from Boomer's coat and stripped it apart. "So why'd you stop doing something that obviously made you so happy?"

"Because I met Anthony, of course." She tried to say it in a blasé tone, but something dark slipped in. She rubbed her shoulder, as though it still ached. "He…swept me off my feet."

"And—"

"I'd rather not talk about him." Her tone grew brittle, and he backed off. Instantly.

"Okay."

Silence swelled between them. Mark waited for her to steer the conversation. How did he make her feel so special? How did he make her believe in him? How did he make her *want* to tell him things?

No one could carry this burden for her, but Mark gave her the feeling that he was willing to help share the load. That in itself was frightening, especially given her traitorous feelings for him. Still, she sighed and said, so softly he had to lean closer to hear, "He was a doctor. Divorced. Passionate. Very territorial. I should have known better. All the red flags were there."

Gently, Mark pulled her into a hug. If she was stiff at first, he didn't say anything. She slowly relaxed in his arms as he gently dried her tears. How did he know how much she needed that? How much she craved it? "You don't have to say anything more," he said into her hair.

When she pulled back, just enough to see his face, still within his embrace, he was blurry. She tried to smile, but knew the effort was timorous at best. "I was so in love with him, I let him have everything. And then…"

"And then?" he prompted, but only because she needed it.

She pulled away and put a few steps between them. "And then he took everything. It happened slowly, if you're wondering. Like the frog in a pot of water. I didn't even realize until it was too—" She let out a shuddering breath.

Mark shook his head. "I didn't mean to upset you."

"You didn't." She set her hand on his shoulder. "It feels good to talk about it. Even though it's unfair to unload on you."

"Hey," he said, putting his arm around her shoulder and pulling her to his side. "I told you, you can talk to me about anything. That is what friends are for, isn't it?"

Was it? She wasn't sure. She hadn't had real friends for so long—Anthony had chased them all away in his attempts to get her all to himself. But who cared what other people did and didn't do? Mark was selfless and kind, willing to listen to her fears and help her work through her issues. The prospect was… Alluring. Empowering.

They stood there, in warmth and friendship, enjoying each other's presence and a simple human touch as they reveled in Boomer's antics. They both laughed when he lifted his tail, pooped in the straw and then did a little dance in the barnyard as though celebrating his accomplishment.

He was truly endearing, but the real warmth in her heart stemmed from the fact that she'd just made a pretty stunning accomplishment of her own.

She'd never talked about Anthony to anyone other than Gretchen and other survivors. Facing her past was scary, and talking about it was even harder.

But with Mark?

Somehow, Mark made her feel safe.

Chapter Four

It was a challenge for Mark to keep his mouth shut on the topic of Roni's husband. Mostly because the things he wanted to say weren't things that would help the situation any. Besides, what she needed right now was a friend she could confide in, not someone to fight her battles. He wasn't sure why she'd chosen him—he wasn't the kind of man women usually friend-zoned—but he intended to step up to the task.

This just…felt right.

Maybe it was because their friendship had been so firmly cemented in those summers spent together when they were kids, but he *knew* that he wanted—needed—to support and protect her. It was an irrefutable urge. And a frustrating one.

Even though she hadn't given him any specifics about her marriage, he'd been around. He knew to what she was alluding. He knew, from working with abused animals for so long, that what you *saw* was usually only the tip of a very ugly iceberg.

Animal or human, abuse was abuse. People

filled with hate were deeply wounded and, in turn, wounded deeply.

The frustration came along with the urge to heal, to fix something that was sometimes unfixable.

At this moment, he was consumed with a raging desire to put the hurt on Anthony for whatever he'd done to turn the happy girl he remembered into a woman who was afraid to trust her heart and body to anyone ever again. But it wasn't his place to avenge her.

It killed him to imagine what she must have been through. How she'd had to fight to retain those precious pieces of herself. Something whipped through him, some soul-deep feeling… Was it admiration? Or respect? Probably both.

He wished he could open his mouth and say something that could make it all better. Instead, he took her by the shoulders and met her gaze as he said, "I am…proud of you, Roni."

Her expression dissolved into confusion. "What are you talking about?"

How to put it into words? "After everything you've been through… You're still *you*. You didn't let it go."

She shook her head. The motes in the air danced around her head. "What…?"

"Your spark," he said, because he couldn't think of any other word for it. "You didn't let him take your spark." His voice was thick with emotion, and he hadn't realized until this moment just how deeply he'd been affected by everything she'd told him. Not the anger—although he was definitely furious—but sorrow, for her, for what she'd been through. And happiness...because she'd survived. And she'd kept her spark.

"Ah, Roni," he said, because there was nothing else to say, and if there was, he sure couldn't think of it.

She hugged him then, long and hard as such hugs were meant to be.

"Hey, you two," Sam called. Mark whipped around to see his sister, along with Luke, framed in the doorway.

"We came to get you because dinner's ready," Luke added.

Sam set her hands on her hips. "Can you two stop hugging so we can eat already?"

Roni stepped back and smiled at Mark, her eyes shining with appreciation. Her gaze dropped to his chest, and then she patted at a damp spot on his shirt. "Sorry about that," she said. "I guess I got a little emotional."

He curled his arm around her and held her in a side hug as they made their way back into the sunlight. "You don't ever have to be sorry," he said, softly enough that the others couldn't hear. "Not with me."

* * *

Roni's heart ached, but in a good way. She could never have imagined it when Gretchen had initially counseled her about learning from the past and healing. Back then, healing had seemed like an impossibility. And now, here she was, with a full heart.

It felt…lovely.

She was so thankful to Mark for not seeing her as a victim, but it meant even more that he saw her as a fighter.

That he *saw* her.

That meant the world.

She'd been certain that when people found out about her time with Anthony, they wouldn't understand. They might even blame her for letting it happen more than once. Or they'd shy away, because of their own discomfort. But Mark hadn't.

Oh, sure, he didn't know the worst parts—and she had no intention of sharing—but somehow, it didn't matter. He accepted her *unconditionally*.

Right now, that meant more to her than words could say.

Emma ran to them when she saw them emerge from the barn and then blocked their way, standing there, arms akimbo. A ferocious expression wrinkled her button nose. "Where have you been?" she wailed. "I turned around and you were gone."

"We went to see the new calf," Mark said, reaching down and hefting her into his arms.

"Without me?" A dramatic howl.

Mark chuckled. "You saw him this morning, remember?"

"But *I* wanted to show Roni."

"You can show her the kittens," Sam suggested.

Emma put out a lip. "It's not the same." She wriggled to get free and when Mark released her, she ran to Roni, took her hand and peeped up at her with soulful eyes. "Will you sit by me at supper? And tell me all about real school?"

"Absolutely. Anything you want to know."

And, Lord help her, Emma asked *everything.* While the others ate their supper, a thick, juicy roast with fingerling potatoes and a nice fresh salad, Veronica explained about recess, bathroom passes, lesson plans and turtles...because Emma had seen a class on TV that had a pet turtle. She was worried every classroom had them, and she wasn't sure what she thought about them because her doctor had told her that some turtles carried a virus and you had to wash your hands after touching them.

"I had to wash my hands all the time," she confided, "when I was sick."

"I imagine so," Roni said. That afternoon, Lizzie had told her all about Emma's illness and how serious it had been. She gave Emma a side hug. "I'm so glad you're better."

"So are we," Lizzie said with a wide smile at Luke, who blushed.

Roni shot him a curious glance. He cleared his throat, wiped his mouth with a napkin and said, somewhat sheepishly, “It was my bone marrow.”

Ah. No one needed to say anything more. But Emma did, anyway. “He’s got super bone marrow. Look.” She made a tiny muscle with her tiny bicep. “I bet he could cure anything with that bone marrow.”

“Yes,” Roni agreed. “I bet he could.”

“I bet I’m as strong as Uncle Luke now.”

“You look pretty strong,” Luke said with a grin, and Emma preened.

“I could probably do anything now,” she said, looking hopefully at her mom.

Lizzie frowned. “No horse camp until the doctors say okay, young lady.”

“Mo-om!” Clearly that had been what Emma had been angling for.

“Hey, anyone ready for dessert?” Roni asked gustily, if only to distract Emma from her argument.

Mark grinned. “Bring it on.”

“What do we have?” Lizzie asked.

“Well,” Sam said with a flourish. “Our guest, Veronica, baker extraordinaire, has made a selection of amazing treats for us. Come on, Roni, let’s bring them in.”

“I want to help!” Emma jumped up, too, as Roni stood to head for the kitchen. But everyone knew Emma really wanted first pick. No one minded at all.

Oddly enough, once dessert was on the table, conversation stopped. Just a lot of moans and *mmm*s. Roni noticed that the apple pie went first, but the brownies were a close second. Of course, Gram took a bunch of molasses cookies before anyone else could get to them. It was gratifying to see all of them eat her creations with such gusto.

"I'm so glad you liked it," she said when one or another of them would surface to compliment her on this or that.

"How are you not baking for a living?" Danny asked.

Roni blinked. She wasn't sure how to respond. She wasn't actually doing anything for a living right now, other than taking care of Gram. She hadn't had a job in years. And after the last time Anthony put her in the hospital, she'd been busy putting herself back together again, focusing on her healing process and, frankly, not much else.

Suddenly, she realized everyone was staring at her, waiting for an answer. In the end, she simply said, "Thanks. I really do love it."

"Hey," Mark said as he helped himself to another lemon bar. "Didn't that bookstore used to be a bakery way back when?"

DJ stroked his lower lip. "Yeah. I remember Mom taking us there once when we were little."

Sam nodded. "I wonder what happened."

"There was a fire in the kitchen," Dorthea said,

which caused heads to swivel. Neither she nor Gram had said much during the meal, other than to gossip with each other about people they used to know, most of whom were now long gone.

Luke gaped at his grandmother. “What?”

“Isn’t that so, Mildred?” Dorthea asked.

Gram shrugged and took another bite of her cookie. “That was before my time, I’m afraid.”

Dorthea barreled on. “Mmm-hmm. See, Frank Barsoni was having an affair with Sally Winthrop. Well, when old Harley Winthrop found out, he had a fit and went into town to burn the bakery down. They caught him before he could do too much damage, of course, and the fire crew was able to save the building, but it was enough to make Barsoni leave town.” She paused and glanced around at all the stunned faces. “It was in all the county papers.” And then, with a shrug, she returned to her cake.

“Well,” DJ said. “There you go. The bookstore used to be a bakery.”

“Heck, if you made stuff like this, I would drive all the way into town to eat it,” Danny said, snagging a brownie.

Sam’s eyes widened, the way they always did when she had a crazy wild idea. “You should.”

“Hmm?” Roni frowned at her.

“You should make stuff like this. You were saying the bookstore’s struggling.” *Struggling* was such a charming way to put it. “What if you refurbish that back room with ovens, refrigeration, whatever you need, and add a bakery/café to the space?"

It was a great idea. Totally ridiculous, but fun to think about.

"You could do that," Mark, by her side, said softly. "You could totally do that."

She glanced at him and he smiled at her. When he smiled at her, she felt it down to her soul. "It's Gram's store. You all know that, right?"

Gram shrugged. "I love baking. We could work together."

Roni smiled at her. What a lovely thought. Then, of course, reality crashed in. "I don't know the first thing about running a business."

"I do!" Lizzie raised her hand. "I mean, I *am* an accountant. I could advise you."

"She's good," DJ said with a nod.

Still… This was crazy. "Just think how much it would cost to buy restaurant-grade appliances. Not to mention the work that room needs before I could even consider making goods for public consumption. The health and safety inspections we'd have to get—"

"We'll help," Mark said.

His offer was then echoed by each and every one of them.

"You guys are the best. But my point was that the right equipment costs, well, more than I have in my savings."

DJ leaned forward and cleared his throat. "We can help you finance it."

Though warmth swelled, a hint of horror came with it. "I couldn't let you do that, DJ. Businesses fail every day."

"Businesses flourish every day, too," Luke said through a mouthful of brownie.

"This one won't fail. Not in this town." Sam frowned at her. "Have you seen the way these guys eat? And BR is full of people who crave homemade sweets."

Still, Roni resisted. "I don't want to go into debt. It's just not…"

"Tell you what. You can pay us off in baked goods," Mark said.

Danny leaped to his feet. "Better yet, we'll be your partners. Can you imagine? Muffins whenever we want?"

"I make muffins," Lizzie said in a wounded tone.

Danny cleared his throat. "Muffins that aren't made of quinoa."

"Oh, my God. Can you imagine that?" DJ said in a wistful tone.

"No flaxseed?" Mark grinned. "Real butter? I'm drooling."

Lizzie sniffed. "There's nothing wrong with being healthy."

"There is when you want pie." As though to make

his point, DJ took another forkful of the slice on his plate.

Right. It was time to stand up and be firm. All their kindness and generosity was lovely, but it was also making her feel…self-conscious. If she did something like this—and that was a big *if*—she would want to do it on her own terms. Owe no one. "Thank you all for your encouragement. I really do appreciate it. But I just couldn't ask this of you. I really, really couldn't."

DJ studied her for a moment then nodded. "Okay. Just think about it." Which wasn't surrender, exactly, but it was certainly enough to end this uncomfortable conversation.

Though Roni was certain the topic would arise again. She knew this family well enough to expect nothing less.

Mark had a hard time falling asleep that night. Partly because the dogs were hogging the bed, but mostly because he couldn't stop thinking about Roni, running everything she'd told him through his mind over and over again. Thinking about what he might be able to do to help her out.

Of course, his mind wandered to things he could do to make her happy, though he knew in his gut *those* ideas probably wouldn't fly. Of his physical attraction to her, there was no doubt. But she wasn't ready for that, and even he could recognize that she might never be after what she'd been through.

He knew she needed a friend, but it ran deeper than that, he was realizing. She needed at least one man in her life—maybe he could be the first man to do it for her—who would respect her boundaries. Who, in doing so, would be able to help her heal not just whatever physical wounds lingered, but the emotional trauma of her marriage. The confidence and self-worth that had been cruelly stolen had to be restored to her. He couldn't do it for her—he knew that. But maybe, by keeping their relationship platonic, while being present and there for her in ways she required...maybe that would be enough to help her find what she needed.

It wouldn't be easy. The irony wasn't lost on him. When a person is told what they are often enough—when a person fulfills expectations often enough—it becomes a living thing, a reality. Sometimes a cage.

No one had ever expected anything more of him than to be a good-looking guy, out for a good time. He'd delivered exactly that, always being the Mark Stirling everyone expected—smiling, easygoing, constantly up for fun, without a thought in his head. Was it wrong for him to want to be seen as someone capable of so much more than just a good-time Charlie? To be valued for who he was, rather than just what he looked like?

Every romantic relationship he'd ever had, had ended, and all for one reason. They'd been based on the physical…because neither he nor his various partners bothered to reach for something more. And then, when all those couplings based on physical attraction petered out—and they always did, at some point—there was nothing left to cling to. Sometimes he wondered if that might be all he had to offer a woman—sex. Was it foolish to want to be worth more than that to someone?

But now, here he was, faced with a woman who wanted everything from him *except* that. A drop-dead-gorgeous, smart, funny, challenging woman. A woman he wanted physically, but also wanted in a deeper way, in a way he didn't quite understand.

Was this irony or opportunity to prove to himself that he could be more than he was? Or both?

Regardless, he was determined to try. No. He was determined to *succeed* in being a good friend to her. If that was all she was willing to take, then that's what he'd give her.

Hell, it might even be good for him.

Gram went right to bed that night, but Roni's mind was in a whirl after their day at the ranch. She hadn't enjoyed herself so much since…well, she couldn't remember. The whole day, she'd felt warm and welcome and, yes, part of a family.

More so than she'd ever felt with her own family,

but then, Mom and Dad had been too busy fighting with each other to bother much with her. On top of that, living in a military household meant moving every year or so, which made lasting friendships difficult. Her life had had little or no stability whatsoever. Different friends, different schools, different houses. Perhaps that was why summers here had been so special for her. She'd always felt *included* here, a part of something. There had been a consistency she'd never experienced anywhere else.

Was it such a surprise that she'd *thought* she'd found it with Anthony? He'd had a regimental air about him that felt familiar to her. He'd liked order. He'd liked things in their place. He'd liked knowing where she was and who she was with and what she was doing at all times. At first, she'd been charmed by that obsession over her every breath, but after a while, she'd recognized his control for what it was. Malignant.

Every time she attempted to step outside the imaginary walls he had created, she threatened his authority over her. And she paid. The price got higher and higher, until finally it cost her the dream of being a mother.

Granted, she'd only been three months along in her pregnancy, but that hardly mattered. Any woman who'd suffered such a loss would understand. She'd loved that baby with all her heart. She'd built a world of hope and dreams around that baby. Now, because of the damage he'd caused, she'd not only lost her baby, but also, according to the specialists who had treated her injuries, she'd lost any future chance to have children. Ever.

Of all the pain Anthony had caused her in their marriage, that loss was, and always would be, the worst.

It felt so good to be free of him. To be free of the weight of trying to please someone who took pleasure in being displeased. Gretchen said it took courage to release the past, and it was true. It had taken two years, but, damn, if it wasn't worth the effort.

Oh, sure. She still had things to work through, and she knew it. But she also knew she was getting better. She was starting to see the light at the end of the tunnel, and it felt really good.

Roni wasn't tired in the least that night, so she made herself a cup of tea and nibbled on cookies as she watched a rerun of a sitcom on television, and allowed herself to laugh. It wasn't long before her mind took her back to the events of the day. Specifically, in the barn with Mark.

Yes, it had been horrifying to realize that he had found out about the true nature of her marriage. But now, looking back, taking in his reaction to it, and to her, her heart swelled.

He had accepted her, unconditionally. No one had ever done that before. There had always been conditions attached to love in her life, with her parents and with Anthony—conditions like obedience and compliance. So while this feeling was alluring, she was careful not to sink into it.

Oh, it was a blessing—really, it was—to have a friend like him. Mark's support made her so happy she wanted to sing, but that might wake up Gram, so she decided to bake instead.

As she mixed a batch of muffins—with quinoa and flaxseed, just for Lizzie, who was insisting on healthy foods because she was pregnant—Roni hummed beneath her breath. Her thoughts kept straying back to Mark. During their *date* the other night, she'd been sure he'd only given lip service to understanding her, but now, she knew he truly did. That was a warming thought. Though she was determined to keep to her vow and avoid romantic entanglements, she couldn't deny that, when he'd hugged her, she'd felt…something.

She'd hugged Luke and DJ, as well—they'd been warm and comfortable. But Mark's arms around her, his hard chest against her, the scent of his breath… Lordy.

It was hard for her to admit to herself, but she had to.

Mark was hot.

It wasn't just his big bulky biceps, or that sexy scruff on his chin. Or the dimples, or the crooked smile or the dance of mischief in his eyes. It was his soul. His laugh. His sense of humor, which, somehow, melded perfectly with hers. Of all the men she'd ever met, he was, by far, the most attractive, in every sense of the word.

How wonderful would it be to release her fear or her self-preservation, or whatever it was that fueled her reserve? How wonderful would it be to let herself go and let herself enjoy just one kiss? Or even…more?

She froze in the process of slipping the muffins into the oven as a mind-boggling realization hit her. It was deliriously yummy. Warm and liquid and loose. It sent little tingles through her body. It made her want…

How long had it been since she'd even *thought* about that?

From where had this hunger come?

Oh, it hardly mattered.

It was enough to know that she could still have feelings like this. That that part of her hadn't been snuffed out.

The question was, what would she do about it?

When the sun finally rose, Mark pushed the dogs off his legs and got out of bed. After feeding them and letting them out into the run, he dressed and headed up to the house for breakfast. And, frankly, for company. Because if he was being honest with himself, he was feeling a little lonely.

Too bad no one else was around to talk to, so he

grabbed a muffin and headed out to do his morning chores. The minute he was finished, he found himself heading for his truck. Deep in his heart, Mark knew where he was going. He just wasn't sure why.

Before long he found himself parked in front of Milly's bookstore, even though it was still too early for it to be open. Damn—was it too early for Roni to be up? He checked the dashboard clock. He probably should have remembered that not everyone operated on ranch time.

Suddenly, he saw her come through the door that led from her apartment to the store. And his chest grew tight. He sucked in a breath and willed himself to stay calm. What he could not silence was the sudden happiness in his heart. Or the smile that curved his lips when she spotted him, grinned and waved maniacally.

He levered out of his truck and met her at the door. "Good morning," he said as she ushered him inside.

"Good morning," she said cheerfully. "Are you psychic?"

"What?"

Her laugh was like a melody. "I was just thinking about you and here you are. What are the odds?"

What were the odds? Lately it seemed like he was always thinking about her. "What are you doing?" he asked instead.

"Well," she began, "I was up all night thinking

about what you guys said and..." She held up a tape measure. "I thought I'd get a feel for the dimensions. You know, to see how feasible it is to run two businesses here. The bookstore means too much to Gram. I couldn't just take over."

"Of course not."

"But now that I'm down here, I realized how silly it is to do this alone, and Gram is still asleep. Could you help?"

He grinned even wider. "Help you chase this dream? Hell, yeah, I'll help."

She rolled her eyes at him, but couldn't help grinning at his eagerness.

For the next hour or so, he followed her lead as she measured and recorded nearly every square inch of the little store. As they worked, she shared some of the ideas she'd had and they talked them out. He especially liked her idea of giving away samples in advance of the launch. Everyone loved baked goods, and free baked goods were even better!

He really liked her idea of paying him for his labor in cookies.

Ah, but there was a method to her madness. Once she had him installed upstairs at her kitchen table—with a couple of cookies and a glass of milk—she pulled out a rough sketch she'd made of the store and scribbled in the measurements they'd taken.

"What do you think?" she said, sliding the paper over so he could see it better. "This section by the door and along this wall is underused. Gram only uses it for checkout. I could see this whole side refurbished like a café."

Mark nodded. "If you move these bookshelves over here, there would even be room for some tables. Or better yet, add built-in bookshelves along the walls here and here."

The excitement on her face when she looked at him stole his breath. Made his chest hurt a little, too. "Oh, Mark," she said. "That's perfect."

He forced a smile so she wouldn't realize how much her approval had affected him. It made him want to wrap her in his arms and howl with joy. Instead, he fixed his attention on the layout, even though he didn't really see anything but a blur. "It wouldn't be that difficult to make these changes, either," he said. "Luke loves to build things. I bet he'd be all over that."

Why he referred to his brother and his prowess with a hammer at that moment, Mark didn't know, but he was glad he had when her smile widened. "It is possible, isn't it?" she asked.

Her excitement was catching. He put his hand over hers and nodded. "Of course it's possible," he said, ignoring the thudding in his ears. "Anything is possible, if you just don't give up. And like we said yesterday, we're all here to help you."

She set her other hand on his; it was warm. "You're right." And then she leaned closer, causing his heart to skip, because she might have been leaning in to give him a kiss. But she didn't. She said, "I can do this. I can. Thank you, Mark."

Something caught in his throat. "You're welcome."

She returned her gaze to the plans and her smile blossomed. "Oh, Mark. This is going to be so much fun!"

Chapter Five

After Mark headed back to the ranch, Roni was filled with excitement and ideas for the bakery, and, thanks to his suggestion, she decided to talk to Luke to see if he would be willing to help her with some of the carpentry work. He'd seemed supportive yesterday, but he hadn't said much at all. His had been a discernable silence within a tornado of chatter… at least to her. Granted, he'd always been a little different from the rest of the family, although she couldn't put her finger on why. She felt called to reconnect with him and reestablish the friendship they'd had as kids, and to see if he was interested in helping with the bakery; she hoped the spare pan of brownies she'd decided to bring him would serve as an effective bribe.

His place wasn't hard to find, since it was just down the street from the church. It was a humble one-story abode. The yard was spotless and the trim had been recently painted. As she stepped up the stairs to the entry, she heard the strains of Mozart playing.

Mozart? She almost didn't knock, because Luke didn't seem like the kind of guy who went for classical music, so maybe she had the wrong place. She was glad she did when he came to the door. He stared at her for a second, as though it took that long for him to place her, or he was surprised to see her. Then his face broke into a slow grin.

"Roni," he said. "To what do I owe the honor?"

She thrust the pan at him. "I brought you brownies. I noticed they were your favorites last night."

Again, he stared at her a moment too long. "Wow. Thank you so much." He opened the door wider and waved her in. "Come in."

His living room was, in a word, tidy. Not a thing out of place. But that made sense. He'd been a Marine. In the military, order was everything. Her entire life, she'd never seen a cigarette butt on the ground on any base where she'd lived. Litter was unheard of. It was just the culture.

"This is a nice place," she said. And then, when he went to turn off the music, she added, "Please. Leave it on. I love Mozart."

His eyes lit up. "Do you?"

She nodded. "It's great for building new pathways in the brain. I used to play all kinds of classical music when I was teaching. The kids loved it."

He chuckled. "Probably because it's in so many cartoons."

"What's the deal with that?" she asked rhetorically, because no one really knew.

"I started listening as part of my mood therapy after..." His voice trailed off and he shrugged. "Got hooked. Hey, can I offer you a cup of coffee—" he glanced at the pan "—and a brownie?"

"I'd love a cup of coffee. To be honest, the brownies are a bribe."

His brows rose. "Really?"

"Mmm-hmm." She wandered around as he made the coffee, taking in the things he treasured, scattered as they were on the mantel—photos of him in uniform with another man, books on philosophy, a Purple Heart. "I've been thinking about what we were all talking about last night. You know, how everyone liked the idea of turning the bookstore into a bakery. I'd love to have your help, if you're interested. Mark says you're an excellent carpenter."

"Huh." He poured them both a cup of coffee, got the cream from the fridge and brought it over. "Well, I'm happy to help in any way I can."

"Thank you." She reached out and touched his arm. When he jerked back, she could tell it was an instinctual move. "Sorry," she said. "I shouldn't have done that."

He shook his head. "No. I'm sorry. It was just a surprise."

"PTSD?"

He blinked. "I, ah..."

"I recognize the look." As a military brat, she was familiar with post-traumatic stress disorder. Besides, she'd learned to live with it herself.

His expression sobered and he nodded. "I see it in your eyes, too. Some kind of…pain."

She forced a grin. "Do you mean as though life has knocked me on my ass and I'm still trying to figure out how to get back up?"

His smile was warm, sincere. "Something like that."

"I've been through the mill," she admitted. "So have you, I understand."

He grunted. "Heard about that, did you?"

"Not much. Sam mentioned you were injured in the Marines."

"Yeah. An IED got me." He gestured to his left flank, his arm, his leg. "Here. And here."

"I'm so sorry."

He nodded. "They said I'd never walk again."

She caught and held his gaze. "Me, too."

His expression made clear he understood completely, though he took a minute to respond. "Not an IED, I'm guessing."

She hesitated, then confessed, "No. A man."

He went still. His jaw flexed. "I'll kill him."

Her heart pinged. How wonderful did it feel to have a big strong Marine like Luke Stirling offer to avenge her? Even though vengeance was a moot point. What really mattered was having his support.

When she hugged him, it was awkward at first, because he resisted. He clearly wasn't used to spontaneous emotion, or being touched, that much was clear. Well, neither was she. Both of them ignored the tears in their eyes.

When she stepped back, he left his arm around her. It lacked the little sparks she felt when Mark touched her, but it was very comforting.

Was this what having a brother was like?

She and Luke had been friends almost as long as she and Mark had—ever since the day she learned Luke was struggling with his reading, and had helped him with the alphabet. Come to think of it, that's probably when she decided that teaching was what she wanted to do with her life. Funny how one little interaction could set a lifetime course.

He chuckled. "Next thing you know we'll be showing each other our scars."

"Oh?" She turned to face him with a teasing grin. "Is that a Marine thing?"

"Kinda. See?" He stepped back and pulled up his T-shirt, revealing a savage speckling of puckered skin along his flank. "Shrapnel."

"Ouch!" she said. Then, when he looked at her expectantly, she blurted a laugh. "I'm not showing you my scars." She'd never shown anyone who wasn't wearing a white coat and a stethoscope. "But in the interest of friendly competition..." She drew a line along the upper arm of her sweater. "Plate glass shower door."

"Yikes." Though the smile stayed in place on his face, she noticed that the muscles around it tightened. "So where is this Prince Charming? Not that I plan to find him and beat his face into a pulp or anything."

She loved that he didn't ask the terrible question, the one she'd learned to dread. *Why did you stay?* There was no real answer to that. "He's in Walla Walla."

"Really?" Luke's brow furrowed. His smile was wicked. "My favorite prison town. How long does he have?"

She shot him a matching smirk. "Two to five."

Luke's eyes narrowed. "Two to five years? Is that all?"

"Two counts of assault and battery. Yep." She didn't mention the count of involuntary manslaughter, because she really didn't want to talk about that...ever. She had no idea how she managed to be so blasé, other than the fact that she was talking to Luke, who, bless him, empathized without a lick of pity.

Because he'd been there.

She wished she could be sure that Mark would react the same way to the savagery of her truth. But she was too afraid to take that risk, which was why she'd do whatever it took to put off this conversation with him for as long as possible.

Forever, preferably.

Later that evening, Roni had just hung up from her check-in with Gretchen—who was very pleased with her progress—when her phone rang again. It rang so infrequently it was almost a surprise.

She accepted the call with a smile. "Hey, Sam!"

"Hey, Roni. How are you doing?"

"Great."

"I was wondering if you'd be interested in getting together for a girls' night out tonight."

"Sure, if we can do it here. I need to keep an eye on Gram."

"I don't need a babysitter," Gram bellowed from the next room.

Sam heard that and laughed. "We can absolutely come there—"

Roni's heart jerked. "We?" Hopefully her voice wasn't too sharp, but if Sam was planning a party, she'd have to opt out.

"Just me and Crystal. We'll bring dinner and wine. All you have to worry about is dessert."

She grinned. "I think I can manage that."

"Great. See you in a bit!"

As she hung up the phone, happiness trilled through her and Roni had to grin. She had friends!

"Sam's coming over," she said as Gram came into the kitchen.

"I don't need a babysitter."

Roni frowned. Had she misunderstood? "Sam's bringing dinner."

"I said, I don't need a babysitter."

"Gram…"

"I know what Gwen and Max think. They think I'm losing it. But I'm not."

"Gram, you keep reorganizing the bookstore."

She lifted a shoulder. "I enjoy my books."

"It's bad for business."

"I don't care about business. I just enjoy my books."

"You see why Gwen is worried about that, right? You own the only bookstore in town but don't care about making money?"

She sent Roni the look—the one Roni remembered from childhood when someone had irritated Gram. "I didn't open the bookstore for money. I just wanted something to do."

"Something to do?"

"Yes." She nodded so definitively the gray curls on her head bounced. "And I love books, so a bookstore made sense. Retired people who have nothing to do are more prone to depression and dementia. I read that in my *AARP* magazine. Oh, I know you kids think I'm all used up, but I'm not."

"No. Of course you're not."

"And at my age, why shouldn't I do what I want?"

An excellent point. "Hmm. Sit down." She pulled out a chair and Gram settled herself at the table. "Do you remember what we talked about at the Stirlings'? About me possibly opening a bakery? How would you feel about that?"

Gram blinked. "Where?"

"Downstairs. In the shop. That side of the store without shelves, by the register, is underused. And that back room full of junk, well, it's big enough to be used as a kitchen. It just needs ovens, a fridge, a freezer. Mark and I have been working on ideas for—"

"Oh. You're doing it with Mark?" Her eyes brightened.

"Well, he's helping. All the Stirlings are. Lizzie's an accountant and she says it's a good prospect, considering the lack of competition. So, what do you think?"

"Oh, I don't know…"

Roni's mood drooped at the hesitancy in her voice. Without Gram's approval, none of this would happen.

Then she shot Roni a glance under her lashes. "What's in it for me?"

Wait. Was this blackmail?

"Um, what do you want?"

Gram looked at her shrewdly. "I like molasses cookies."

She was bargaining? Okay. "If I have a bakery, I'd probably make them more often."

Gram pouted. "I'd think you would make them every day, if you had a bakery to stock."

Roni swallowed a laugh. "Ah—sure, I could make them every day." Yeah. That was doable.

"Well, then," Gram said. "That sounds like a wonderful idea."

Roni pulled out the plans she and Mark had been working on, and she and Gram discussed them in detail until Sam and Crystal showed up bearing homemade lasagna.

She'd met Crystal before, at the B&G, but there hadn't been a chance to get to know her in that hectic environment. Now, over lasagna, garlic bread and wine, she could truly appreciate why she and Sam were friends. Both were funny as all get-out—even Gram laughed at some of their antics—and she knew all kinds of tidbits about the locals, which kept the conversation interesting.

And when it turned to darker topics—after dinner, after Gram had left the table and deep into the second bottle of wine—it became clear that they'd both suffered terrible losses.

Crystal had lost her husband, a soldier just like Roni's dad. He'd died tragically overseas leaving her to raise their son all alone. Like Roni, she didn't have any other family to rely on. Like Roni, she was alone in the world.

Just as Roni was starting to feel maudlin, Gram, wearing her jammies, came into the living room—where they'd migrated after dessert—and kicked them out because her show was on.

Roni bit back a smile. Maybe she wasn't all alone in the world after all. She had Gram. She had Mark. She had friends.

And soon…she'd have a bakery.

The next few weeks were busy and exciting for Roni. The more she thought about the idea of adding a bakery/café to the bookstore, the more she liked it. She could tell the Stirlings did, too—especially when she started testing recipes. One or another of them would stop in to the bookstore every day to say hello and to sample her latest creation. Her favorite days were the ones when Mark came by, although it wasn't nearly as often as she would have liked. She found herself missing him when she didn't see him. Though she knew he had wanted more of her than simple friendship, he never brought up the subject again. He certainly never said or did anything that made her uncomfortable. As a result, their relationship flourished, as it was free from any sexual tension.

Well, there might have been a little sexual tension, but it never got in the way. The fact that said tension didn't all come from Mark was something she tried to ignore. But she couldn't completely disregard the fact that being around him seemed to have awakened something within her. In her efforts to push aside those feelings, she poured all her passion into her work and was happy to do it. Perfectly happy.

And those dreams she was having about Mark? Those were just a result of spending so much time with him. She was certain of it.

Lizzie came by on a regular basis to talk with her about financing, insurance, equipment depreciation and all kinds of other things that made Roni's head spin. Fortunately, Lizzie was used to boiling the details down to their simplest form.

Because Gram owned the building, Roni's biggest expenditures would be renovations, appliances—at least two double ovens and a gas range—baking supplies and advertising. Lizzie drafted a sample budget that even Roni could parse out. It explained how much she needed to bring in to pay off the bank loan, which Roni insisted on getting. She was not taking money from her friends, and that was that.

The challenge after that was sitting down with Ben Nadler, the bank manager, to present her business plan. Lizzie and Mark insisted on going with her, but Roni was certain it was the pastries she brought, made with fresh Rainier cherries, that sealed the deal…not the looming cowboy behind her. Though, to be honest, it didn't hurt that the Stirlings had the most successful ranch this side of the

Columbia River. Mr. Nadler must have been relatively certain he wouldn't be losing anything on this deal with the Stirlings standing behind her. Her loan was approved on the first try.

Sam insisted they not wait until the money came through to start on the to-do list, and organized immediate work parties to clean out and renovate the old kitchen. Gram had been using it as a bolt hole for books she didn't want to put on the shelves, so there were a lot of old romances in there, as well as the occasional murder mystery. Beyond that, they found more shelving, an antique pastry-display case that Luke insisted on refurbishing and a very old but adorable cash register. There were a ton of random items in there, as well, some dating back to the 1920s, including some pretty Depression glass, an old butter churn and a completely rusted egg beater. Some of the items ended up in the dumpster, but Roni salvaged a lot of them, because she knew the antiques would make charming decorations for a bakery.

Word got around town that she was testing recipes, and all of a sudden, the bookshop had visitors aplenty. While she couldn't sell baked goods until her business license, health inspections and insurance came through, she was more than happy to give away samples. And the people of Butterscotch Ridge were more than happy to eat them. Between word of mouth and the excitement of the residents about having an actual bakery in town again, the whole Stirling clan was certain the shop would be a hit, even if it was part bookshop, as well.

Each day, Roni saw her goal coming closer and closer to fruition. It was a wonderful feeling, a spiritual healing, perhaps. She could feel the pieces of herself coming together again, joining, strengthening, flourishing. She felt like her true self again, that person she used to be.

"What are you grinning about?" Mark asked her one day as they finished the second coat of paint. The walls were a beautiful blue—the ceiling, too, because she liked the idea that her bakery might have a sky. The plan was to paint grasses along the bottom and flowers above that. She'd already invited Emma, as well as Crystal and her son to help with that tomorrow.

This growing friendship with Crystal was another thing that was new to Veronica, and made her feel so good. Crystal was funny and smart and talented; they'd just...clicked. Same with eight-year-old Jack, whom Roni found endearing.

She glanced at Mark, standing by the back wall with a roller in his hand. And she had to grin. "You're dripping," she said on a laugh.

He looked down and grimaced when he saw spots of blue on his boots. He dropped the roller into the pan. "At least I don't have blue freckles," he said as he made his way over the tarp toward her. "How about a break? I could use a rest."

"I do not have blue freckles," she insisted, and laughed again.

He shrugged and grinned. "If you say so." He said this with a tone that made her wonder if she did, indeed, have paint on her face. "Didn't you say you made lunch?" He opened the cooler she'd set by the door and riffled through it, then pulled out wrapped sandwiches and chips and said triumphantly, "Ta-da!"

"It's not lunchtime yet," she reminded him.

He chuckled. "I'm a growing boy. Come on. Let's sit outside. It's a nice day."

It was a beautiful July day, with cool breezes and sunshine. They'd put the bistro table and chairs outside during the painting. She liked the look of it so much she started thinking about getting another, and leaving them outside for customers to enjoy on days like this one. She nodded. "Yes. Let's."

They'd barely taken a seat when he returned to his earlier question. "What were you grinning at before?"

She unwrapped her PB&J and frowned at him. "I'm supposed to remember?"

"It was a pretty big grin."

"Nothing really," she said as she watched the activity on Main Street. There wasn't a lot, but she liked it that way. A robin flew down and inspected the sidewalk in front of them for crumbs. "I was just thinking about how happy I am right now." Sitting there, with him. Soaking in the summer sun. "Hopeful, too."

"Hopeful?" He took a swig of his soda. "Hopeful for what?" His expression sobered. "What are you looking for? In life?"

"Wow. That's a big question." She paused and thought for a minute. "I think what I need to be happy is to feel safe. Warm. Protected—"

He chuckled. "Sounds like you need a German shepherd."

She waggled a finger at him. "I see what you're doing there," she said playfully. "When I'm ready for a dog, trust me, I'll let you know."

His grin made it clear he was not chagrined.

"Besides, I wasn't done. I also need this." She waved at the store. "A purpose." She pushed back her bangs when the breeze teased them into her face. "What about you? What do you want?"

He flinched. "This is where I say I have the perfect life, isn't it?"

Something in his tone caught her attention, prompted her to ask, "Is it?"

Mark traced the beads of condensation on the soda can. He blew out a deep breath. "It should be. Shouldn't it? I love my work. Love my dogs. Love my family…"

"But?"

His barked laugh was bitter. “But…I can’t help wondering if there’s something more. Something I’m missing.” She hated the murky look in his eyes. She wanted to wipe it away, but she didn’t know how.

“I feel that way, too, sometimes,” she said. “I think everyone does.”

He raked back his hair. “Right, but then I think, how dare I want more when I already have so much? When some people have nothing?”

“It’s not a competition. You can’t compare yourself to other people, though I know the temptation is pretty great sometimes. Besides…” She had to clear her throat because something there was clogged. “There’s nothing wrong with seeking fulfillment, no matter how blessed you are.”

“I know.” He sat back, as though the conversation was over, but then he added, in a softer tone, “Sometimes I wonder…” He trailed off.

She frowned. “Wonder about what?”

His sigh was heavy. “Never mind.”

Really? She glowered at him. “You can’t just bring something up and then just leave it lying there like that.” And then, when he didn’t cave, she crossed her arms and huffed. “I told you my dark secrets. It’s only fair that you tell me yours.”

“It’s not a dark secret.” True. Nothing about him was dark. That was one of the things she liked about him. “It’s just…dumb.”

“I can handle dumb. Come on.”

It took a while for him to find the words. To encourage him, she handed him a cookie, even though he hadn't finished his sandwich. It was chocolate chip, his favorite. More hopeful birds gathered.

Mark ate half of the cookie before he spoke. "Okay. You know that my parents both died when I was young. My granddad raised me."

She nodded. "I remember him. He let me drive the tractor once."

"Yeah. He was…different with girls." His lips dipped in the corners.

"What do you mean?"

"Sam couldn't do anything wrong. We—the boys—couldn't do anything right."

"I am so sorry."

"There was more to it than just that. The fact is, Granddad wasn't a very…warm person. There was no hugging when we were kids. And he was very strict. His expectations were high. We were Stirlings, damn it. Things were expected of us. There was always this constant pressure to please him."

"Huh," she said noncommittally, but inside, she was having serious déjà vu. It had been like that with Anthony, that skulking dark cloud blackening the horizon, that sense that if you weren't perfect, your world would come crashing down upon you. And it sometimes did.

"I wonder…"

"What?" She set her hand on his. She had to. She

needed the connection and she suspected he did, too. Indeed, his fingers closed over hers.

He drew in a deep breath. "I wonder if I'm… damaged. Emotionally. If *we're* damaged. You know. Me and my siblings."

Roni shook her head. "You seem very loving, very warm with each other. You know, I always envied you your relationships." She always had. As an only child, she'd craved a family like theirs.

"Yeah, but look at us. Danny's the only one who's taken that risk, and he didn't grow up in that house. He never even met the old man."

"Is that why you never got married?" It was a blurted question. It just slipped out. But, in truth, it had been trying to slip out for a while. He was as close to perfect as she could imagine. Why hadn't someone snapped him up?

"You mean, am I incapable of love?" Again, his tone was bitter.

"I don't think that at all. How could I?"

"Well, I do. I wonder. I've dated a lot of women." This he said sheepishly. It wasn't a boast. "I kept looking for this magic feeling, but it was never there. And then…"

This time when he paused, she thought he might not continue. He took another deep breath. It bothered her that he turned away. That he couldn't even look at her as he spoke. "Sometimes I wonder if it's even possible for anyone to want me. I mean, what do I bring to the table? What do I have to offer anyone?"

Her heart jerked. Not from his words as much as the pain in his voice. "You're more than just a pretty face," she said with a grin.

"Am I? I'm not so sure."

"Mark, look at you. You foster abused dogs. You're a volunteer firefighter. You help other people… You're a wonderful person. You would be lovable on any planet."

"Well, I appreciate that. I do. It doesn't change that feeling, though."

"The feeling that something's missing?"

"Yeah. And that, well, maybe there's something's wrong with me, too."

"I don't think there is anything wrong with you. And it's pretty clear to me that it's love you're looking for. That's what's missing."

He frowned at her. "What is love? I mean, what is it, really?"

What was it? And was she qualified to provide any answers on the topic? "I suppose it's a combination of physical, emotional, intellectual and sexual attraction."

"Aren't physical and sexual attraction the same thing?"

She chuckled. "How like a man to ask. There are, in my humble opinion, subtle differences between the two. For example, you can be attracted to someone and not want to jump their bones."

She didn't understand the look he gave her, but he nodded and tersely offered, "True." Silence fell as they munched on their sandwiches and chips. Then he said, more to the begging birds that had surrounded them than to her, "How do you know you're in love, anyway? How do you know if a person really loves you?"

She finished her sandwich and shook out the paper, causing a flutter in the flock. "Maybe the lady with the failed marriage isn't the one to ask," she said on a sigh. "With Anthony, it was his devotion that convinced me he loved me. He showered me with what I thought was love. But it wasn't. With the benefit of hindsight, and therapy, I can see now that it was just…bait." She sighed. "Marriage—heck, love—should be a partnership. An equal partnership. But if you want love in your life, Mark, you have to open up to it. You have to take a gamble sometimes."

"Yeah," Mark said as he started cleaning up their mess. "I think you're right. Love is a gamble."

Roni nodded. "And when you gamble big and lose, you aren't that anxious to try again."

"I can think of one way to make sure you never lose."

"Never play?"

He shook his head. "Nope." His grin was mischievous. "You stack the deck."

Stack the deck? She had to laugh; he was just too dang adorable. If she could figure out how to do that, she probably would try.

Mark stayed for supper. Gram enjoyed the company because he was such a good listener. Roni found herself watching him and marveling at how good he was with Gram. When she told the same story three times about the book she'd thought she'd lost, he encouraged her as much as he had the first time. When she occasionally called him Daniel—his father's name—he didn't correct her. He was too kind to do so.

It was hard for Roni to watch him leave that night. Hard to watch the taillights of his truck diminish in the dark from her little balcony. Partly because she hated it when he left, and partly because, it was times like this, in the quiet of the night, that it hit her.

That hollow loneliness.

Yes, things were wonderful. Her future was bright. But she couldn't help but think ahead to a day when Gram would be gone and she would be occupying this apartment, all alone. Living by herself. There would be times like this, wouldn't there? Where she wished she had someone by her side? When she didn't want to be alone?

Brutally, she pushed such gloomy thoughts from her mind. Her decision to remain single was the right thing. She wasn't in the frame of mind to let a man share her life. Falling in love again might break her.

The fact that Mark was such a wonderful person lured her into dangerous thoughts. Not to mention those tantalizing trills that ran through her belly when his hand happened to graze hers. Or when their eyes met with a certain intent. Or when he breathed…

Maybe she should stop spending so much time with him.

The moment the thought popped into her head, she rejected it. Nope. The prospect of not seeing him, of excluding him from her life, was unthinkable. Her heart leaped every time she spotted him. He stirred excitement in her soul. Their time together was easy and they could talk about anything, even the dark things, as they had today.

She did care about him—there was no doubt about that. But as a friend. And she was fairly certain he felt the same way about her, too. She and Mark shared a platonic relationship, a safe relationship… Well, other than the feelings of arousal he could raise in her with a look. And the dreams. And the daytime fantasies.

It nearly broke her heart when he'd told her he worried that he might be damaged, because she could relate to such a fear, though she *knew* she was damaged. She'd known for a while. Thinking of it made her want to just hold him. Made her want to prove to him that he was worthy, and deserving, of love.

But she didn't dare.

She pushed away those tantalizing thoughts. It was stupid to even think about. She could not be the one to heal him. She needed her freedom, desperately. The thought of commitment terrified her.

But the thought of being alone terrified her, too.

Surely those weren't the only two options. Surely there was something…in between. If only she could figure out what it was.

For the next couple of months, Mark spent a lot of time with Roni. Certainly enough to test his determination to *just be friends*. While it was getting harder and harder to keep feelings of passion at bay, he had to admit he enjoyed their friendship more than he'd ever thought possible, platonic though it was. Just being with her made him happy.

He woke up as excited as all get-out on the last Saturday in August, because he knew he was going to spend most of the day with her. He'd volunteered his truck for her big shopping trip to the Tri-Cities. She needed to pick up bulk baking goods and some of the equipment she'd ordered, and her car wasn't big enough for everything. He'd been ecstatic to have a chance to spend hours alone with her. He was a little nervous, too, but it was a nervous excitement.

The plan was that Roni would bring Milly over

to the ranch to spend the day with Dorthea while they were gone.

When he heard Emma excitedly calling out to Roni—because, of course, she'd been watching for her—he headed to the front door, where he spotted her helping her grandmother out of the car.

Roni glanced up and smiled at him. And stole his breath.

Damn, she was gorgeous. It was funny the way it surprised him sometimes, just how beautiful she was. He could stare at her forever and never get bored. He forced a friendly grin as she led Milly up the stairs. "You look great!"

"Well, thank you," Milly said.

Roni knew his comment was for her so she chuckled. "Thanks. Lizzie has me eating kefir and drinking kombucha."

Mark made a face. "You better be careful around her. She's a health-food fanatic."

Roni shrugged. "But it feels so good."

"You're not turning vegan, are you?"

Her grin broadened. "And give up bacon candy?"

Mark pretended to drool as he held the door for them. "Will you be selling bacon candy at the bakery? Think how many customers you'd wrangle."

She chuckled. "Well, we'd better wait and see how the bakery fares before we turn to bacon for rescue."

"Everybody loves bacon."

She waggled a finger. "Not vegans."

"In case you haven't noticed, there aren't very many vegans in this town." To which they both laughed. This was beef country, after all.

"I love bacon," Emma said, in an attempt to win Roni's attention, which, of course, she did.

"Well," Roni said, going down on her knees to hug her, "I'll make some bacon candy just for you, then."

"Will you really?"

"Of course."

Emma threw her arms around Roni's neck and squeezed with all the enthusiasm a six-year-old bacon lover could muster. As Mark watched them together, something caught in his throat. It was such a sight, these two females he adored hugging in a shaft of sunlight.

A vision popped into his head—absolutely unexpectedly—of Roni with a daughter, a little redhead with curly hair and his dimples. It made his knees weak. It made him...want. It made him want something he wasn't supposed to want.

He pushed it away, that vision. He had no claim to it. And he had no idea why it cut so deep. With effort, he forced a nonchalant expression. "Have you had breakfast?" he asked as they led Milly into the parlor, where his grandmother awaited her visitor.

"There's bacon," Emma announced.

Roni grinned at her. "Oh, nummy. Too bad I already ate." She checked her phone. "We should probably get going so we don't get back too late."

"Okay." Mark made sure Milly was seated, kissed both grandmothers on the forehead and turned back to the foyer. But someone stood in his way. Someone short. She had her arms crossed and wore a mutinous expression.

"I want to go, too."

He kneeled down and put his nose to Emma's. "You can't come, munchkin. This is going to be a long day."

Emma frowned. Fiercely. "But I'm better now. I can do long days."

By now, Mark was quite experienced with precisely how stubborn his niece could be, but less experienced at winning negotiations with her. So he was relieved to see Lizzie coming down the stairs. "Not today, Ems. I need your help."

She whirled and turned her frown on her mother. "But I want to go with them."

"We can go another time. Today, we're planning a very special tea party for the grandmas, and I need your help. You're the best scone maker, right?"

Oh, the conflict warring on her on her tiny face was priceless. The tea party won out. "Oh, all right," she said on a huff.

Lizzie nodded to Mark. "You two better go," she warned. Her tone made it clear that Emma could change her mind at any second, so they did not delay. Mark mouthed a silent thank-you as he passed and Lizzie grinned. "You owe me," she said, *sotto voce*.

He didn't bother to ask her what for. That much was already clear.

"Are you ready?" he asked Roni, though it was a purely rhetorical question.

"Let's hit it."

As he helped her into his truck, he said, "Maria asked if we could stop at the flea market in Pasco and pick up some corn husks. I hope you don't mind. Apparently she's planning to make tamales tomorrow, and they have the ones she likes." Maria had taken over Gram's job as the Stirling housekeeper and cook when she'd retired; now that his grandmother was getting older, Maria helped take care of her, too.

"Of course I don't mind."

He closed her door, jogged around to the driver's side, heaved in and tried to catch her gaze before he started the truck. Just a smile, nothing much, but she wasn't paying attention to him.

She pulled out her shopping list and silence reigned until they reached the end of the long driveway. It was kind of awkward, because they'd never experienced a lack of things to say to one another. She probably had a lot on her mind, given the impending grand opening and all, but he sensed a tension in her that made him uneasy. He wished he could figure out what it was.

"Thanks so much for driving me," she said, at long last.

"Sure." Was that all he could think of to say?

"Your truck is so much bigger than my car."

He shot her a grin. "Well, that's what friends are for." Because they were friends. Even though he had to occasionally remind himself.

"About that..."

Something in her tone caught his attention. Something twanged in his solar plexus. He tried not to stare at her, on account of the fact he was driving and all. "Hmm?" Yeah. Pretty much all he could manage.

"I mean I've been wondering... Oh, I don't know how to say this."

"Just say it." What on earth was bothering her? Why was it so hard to get it out? "We're friends, right? There's nothing we can't talk about."

She turned to him, her eyes wide. "You mean that?"

"Of course I mean it." He wasn't sure why, but his pulse pounded like a big bass drum.

"Maybe you'd better pull over."

Well, *that* didn't sound good. He eased the truck to the side of the highway and shifted so he could see her better without cricking his neck. "What is it, Roni?"

Yikes. She was twisting her fingers and everything. A sure sign she was really bothered. She took a deep breath before she spoke. “Well, you know how I told you I wasn’t interested in romance?”

His heart hiccuped. “Yeah?”

“Well, I’m still not. But…”

“But?”

She met his gaze. A flush rose on her cheeks. “Do you think it’s possible for friends to have sex and stay friends?”

Chapter Six

Mark's jaw dropped. Whatever he'd been anticipating, it definitely wasn't *that.* "Ah…you mean like friends with benefits?"

Roni frowned. "I know what it's called. I don't like that term."

He nodded. "Okay. We can call it something else."

For some reason, she ignored his brilliant suggestion. "That's not the point."

"No?" He huffed a little laugh. "I may be missing the point. I'm a little distracted right now."

She blew out an exasperated breath. "I'm asking if you think it's possible. I mean, for friends to have sex without ruining their relationship."

"I think that depends on the people."

That answer seemed to frustrate her more, but he really didn't know what to say or how to respond to this topic…mostly because he had no idea what she was really driving at. She gored him with an intense look that insinuated he should.

"Do you think people can have that kind of relationship without one person becoming possessive? Thinking they own the other?"

"Is that what you think romance is?" he asked. "People owning each other?"

"Of course. It's just natural. It's the way men are."

He blanched. "It's not the way men are." Then, realizing his blunder, he reconsidered. "Well, some men. But *not* all men, Roni. I'm certainly not like that."

"So you don't feel possessive over women you date?"

"I'm a bad example." True, he'd never felt a hint of possessiveness for any of the women he'd dated, because he'd known they weren't the one. They weren't his *other*. He refused to explore how he felt about Roni, because he knew in that expedition lay danger. "But, yes, some men feel possessive." And then he added, "But that's a far cry from what you experienced with Anthony. That wasn't a healthy relationship, Roni. I may not know everything about love and marriage, but I know that much."

"I see." She seemed preoccupied with her swirling thoughts, so when she suggested they keep going, he started the truck and continued down the long two-lane highway into town, even though he was bursting with questions.

It wasn't long before she turned back to him and asked, "So what do you think about friends with benefits?"

He nearly crashed the truck, but using his advanced truck-handling experience, and the fact that, aside from them, the road was empty, he managed not to. "What do *I* think about it?" He didn't, truth be told. It had been a long time since he'd been interested in casual sex, despite what his friends thought of him.

"Yeah. Do you think it's a good idea?"

How could he say no when he had a pretty good idea where this was going? "Look, Roni, I think each relationship is different, because the people are different. The most important thing is to be honest with each other and be respectful of the other's feelings. If you do that, it's kind of hard to screw it up."

Her laugh was bitter. "People screw it up every day."

"Because they break those rules, I'd guess. Or the passion fades."

"And what happens then?"

He had to glance at her. Thank God they were on a straight portion of highway at the moment. "Then it ends, I guess. That goes back to respecting each other's feelings. Relationships are a two-way street."

This time, it didn't take her long to speak up again at all. "It wasn't a two-way street with Anthony."

"No. It wasn't. And the idiot lost you because of it."

A heavy silence fell and he kicked himself for saying the wrong thing. But then, she laughed. It was a bitter but beautiful laugh. Beautiful, because it was at Anthony's expense. "Yes, he did, didn't he?"

"A man who really respects you and cares for

you would never hurt you. When you're in a real relationship, a healthy relationship, you are equals."

"Do you really believe that?"

He nearly snorted. "Of course I do! Besides, a woman I respect very much told me exactly that. Just a few days ago, in fact. Marriage is a partnership—I believe she said something like that."

A pink tinge rose on her cheeks. He wasn't sure if it was pleasure that he'd been listening or embarrassment of some kind, but it didn't much matter. She pursed her lips. "A lot of men are chauvinists."

Chagrin lanced his heart. "You know I'm not a chauvinist, right?"

"I know you're not an Anthony."

And, to be honest, that was all that really mattered, wasn't it?

They decided to stop at the Pasco Flea Market to grab Maria's corn husks before picking up the perishables for the bakery. Besides, Mark said he was hungry and there was amazing food at the pop-up Mexican market. It was unlike anything Roni had ever seen in Seattle. Located in an enormous dirt lot, the market consisted of vendor after vendor selling everything from corn husks—which they bought right off the bat so they didn't forget—to clothing, to electronics, to churros.

The churros, which cost a dollar each, were warm and delicious and freshly fried. Mark, thinking ahead, bought extras and they nibbled the cinnamon, sugar-coated treats as they wove through the crowds wandering along row upon row of booths.

"It's like a maze in here," Roni said as they passed what she was certain was the same stall selling belts and leather goods for the third time.

"Mmm. I love it. Can you hear the music?"

She made a face at him. "Who *can't* hear the music?" Because no fewer than three different songs blared from three different directions.

"And smell that. Is that fajitas?"

"Didn't you just eat your third churro?" She had to tease him, although now she understood why he'd bought so many.

"Listen, I don't get out much. Let me have some fun."

And, apparently, his idea of fun was eating Mexican food from an outdoor stand while listening to mariachi music as the sun beat down on their heads. As they finished their lunch, Roni watched children dancing to the music and eating enormous ice-cream cones.

Come to think of it, it was a pretty cool experience. Oh, it was hardly a fancy place—the bathrooms probably dated from the fifties, electrical cords dangled down from the tent poles and, where the dirt was muddy, they'd covered it with mismatched boards—but she loved it.

Mark finished his fajitas and crumpled up his trash. "We should probably go."

She followed his lead. “Okay, but I want to find something for Emma.” So on the way back to the truck, she stopped at a booth selling *Frozen* paraphernalia and bought Emma a backpack for her first day at school, which was coming up soon.

“Aww,” Mark said when he saw it. Then he draped his arm around her shoulder and they made their way through the maze of stalls to the exit. They only got lost once, and that, Roni suspected, was because Mark wanted another churro.

All in all, it was a lovely way to spend the afternoon with a friend…even though it was getting harder and harder for her to think of him as just a friend. Still, she didn’t bring up the subject that had been nagging at her again, but only because she didn’t want to spoil things. Certainly not because if they talked about it outside of the truck, she’d have to make eye contact.

As Mark loaded the equipment and baking supplies for Roni’s new venture into the back of his truck—which was a *Tetris*-like challenge—he couldn’t ignore the warm feeling in his chest. He couldn’t think of anything he’d rather do than spend a day like this with Roni. He enjoyed her company immensely, and she seemed to feel the same way.

She didn’t bring up the subject of friends with benefits again, a fact he faced with mixed emotions. On the one hand, he was dying to pursue the topic and had a multitude of questions churning in his mind. Sure, he was wildly attracted to her and so many of his thoughts wandered to the image of them in bed together—which he struggled to shake off. But he knew she wasn't ready for that yet. If and when she was, she would lead them there.

If, indeed, she chose him to.

In light of all of this, his instincts told him to relax and wait for her to bring it up again when she was ready.

Though he knew the gist of what she'd been through, he had to acknowledge that he really didn't know all that much…other than the fact that he wanted to wipe the tears from her eyes and the pain from her soul. But how? He wished he knew.

"All done!" she chirped as she handed him the last of the boxes, this one holding a variety of flavored syrups.

Mark looked at the jammed truck bed and chuckled. "We can put this box in the cab."

"Perfect. I can't believe it all fit." She grinned at him. "You're awesome."

"I know." He grinned back as he hefted the clunky box into the back seat of the crew cab. "Just so you know, you owe me a beer for this."

She wrinkled her nose. "How about a beer cake instead?" she asked as he came around to slam the tailgate.

"Is that a thing?"

Her laugh was a melody. "This is the twenty-first century. Everything is a thing."

"I think I'd like to try a beer cake," he said as he helped her up into the passenger seat.

"I'll get right on it."

By the time he came around to the driver's side, she'd already found a recipe on Google. As they made their way out of town and back onto the long boring stretch home, they chatted comfortably about beer cake, apple cake, angel food cake and, frankly, all kinds of cake.

He had the sense that she was stuffing the conversation—the way a pastry chef stuffs an éclair—to avoid talking about something else.

And again, he let it go.

She would bring it up again when she was ready.

They were about halfway home—the conversation about cakes having waned—and they were both suffused in silence watching the late-afternoon sun send shards through the clouds, when she finally spoke again. Her question sent a bolt of electricity down his spine.

"Do you remember what we were talking about on the way into town?"

"How bad do you think my memory is?" he asked with a grin.

Her fingers started twisting again. "Well…I wasn't completely honest with you."

Crap. "Ah. So there's more to this, then?"

She glanced at him beneath her lashes. "It's just that… Well, I might have had a couple of…dreams. About you."

It took some effort, but he didn't drive off the road. "What?" Well, hell. Maybe this wasn't the right moment to be *on* the road. He pulled onto the shoulder and put the truck in Park. He had to, for this conversation.

And God, her eyes shone in the twilight.

"What are you saying, Roni?"

She sucked in a deep fortifying breath. "Mark, I am attracted to you. A lot. And I think you are attracted to me—"

"A lot." And, yeah, she smiled at that.

"I would, um, really like to explore this. Us." And, as though to make sure he understood completely, she added, "A friends-with-benefits kind of thing. But with us."

Holy hell. How did a guy respond to that? Well, he knew what he would usually have done—gone right in for a kiss. But this was Roni. He knew better than to do anything he might usually have done with any other woman. Especially considering his track record for long-lasting and fulfilling relationships. One he did not particularly care to repeat. Especially with her.

Instead, he took her hand, which prompted her to continue. "I have to admit, I'm a little scared about the whole thing." Scared or not, she held his gaze.

"You don't ever need to be scared with me, Roni. Just tell me what you want and it's yours."

She stared at him for a minute. Even though the cab was darkening, he could see the flush rise on her cheeks. "Even if it's just a booty call?"

Wow. Talk about a slap in the face. And not quite what he'd expected.

Okay, maybe kind of what he should've expected, but still. "Only if it's a booty call between friends. You see..." He trailed off, but only so he could gather his thoughts. "Even though we've only been, ah, reacquainted for a short while since you returned, our friendship really does mean a lot to me. *You* mean a lot to me. I don't want to do anything to screw it up."

Her eyes lit up. "Yes. You see? That's exactly what I've been worried about."

He had to smile. "I know the feeling."

"Do you think perhaps we could...?"

"Could what?" He was trying not to seem so eager, trying not to rush her, but this conversation was getting difficult. For a lot of reasons.

"Could we set boundaries? So we both understand what this is?"

"Sure." *Yup, sure, absolutely. When?* "Um... What do you have in mind?"

"Well, I'm not interested in marriage, or commitment, or any forever thing. I'd want to keep expectations at a minimum. If we do pursue this, I want you to know what you're getting into. I don't want you to regret being with me—"

"How could you think I would?"

"Let me finish. Please."

"Sorry."

"I don't want to lead you on. I don't want you to think this thing is something it's not. Mostly, I don't want either of us to feel trapped or get hurt. Do you think those are terms you could live with?"

"Yes."

"All right then." She drew in a deep breath, took his hand and stared into his eyes. "Mark Stirling, would you be my friend…with benefits?"

"I will." He held her gaze as he said it. A shudder wracked him.

How ironic that this was a vow of *non*commitment.

Most men would be over the moon.

"Shall we begin now?" she asked.

His mind blanked out. His lungs froze.

Once his brain started working again, he had to laugh, even though this was no laughing matter. Then again, it kind of was. "There are eggs in the back," he reminded her.

Her eyes widened playfully. "What? What do eggs have to do with it? Have I been doing it wrong?"

He chuckled. "Let's unload everything first, shall we?"

"Yes. Yes. Excellent idea."

"And then, we can go upstairs to your apartment—" where there was a bed "—and, ah, finish this conversation there. Okay?"

"Okay," she said. He started the truck, and she folded her fingers and set them in her lap.

Mark could barely focus on the stupid road. It was the longest drive of his life.

Of course, in this case, it was a good thing, because he was able to remind himself how important it was that he did this right. Not just that he remembered to be safe, but that he remembered to be gentle.

The bottom line was that he should avoid doing anything that scared her, or anything she didn't like. He wanted her to feel so good that it made her forget the pain she'd endured with Anthony.

Hell, he'd do anything to make her forget Anthony. Period.

Roni watched the darkening fields flick by, more excited than she'd ever been in her life.

She was going to sleep with Mark Stirling. The thought would have petrified her just a couple of months ago, but right now, she knew she was ready. And she knew he was the right man to escort her on this journey. He was friendly, warm, patient and sweet. He was her friend, and cared about her…but wouldn't expect more than she was willing to give.

He was everything she needed.

She—

"Oh, no."

Mark shot her a look. "What's wrong?"

"I forgot about Gram."

"Text Sam that we're going to be delayed, and have Milly spend the night."

Her heart lurched. "Spend the night?" Did that mean he was going to spend the night, too?

How did she feel about—

Hah. She knew damn well how she felt about that. She tapped in a message to Sam, who quickly responded, Yikes. No problem at all.

When they got back to town, they worked in silence unloading everything from his truck into the refurbished kitchen, and while she appreciated time to prepare for what was coming, it also provided a chance for second thoughts to sprout.

Oh, her proposition hadn't been a momentary whim. She'd thought about it long and hard. She knew this was more than something she wanted. It was something she needed…to heal. The second thoughts came from fear, and she refused to let fear rule her anymore. So when the truck was empty and all the perishables were safely in the fridge—and she'd done a quick tidy-up of all the boxes and bags and wiped down the counters even though they were spotless—she shot him a chipper smile. She didn't exactly make eye contact, but considering the situation, she was sure he would forgive her. "Shall we go upstairs?"

"Sure." He clapped his hands together to indicate he was finished with his chore. Or ready for the next one. "After you."

She led the way up the stairs, barely able to contain her breath. They were actually going to do this. Her heart rattled like a jackhammer. Beads of sweat prickled at her nape.

How long had it been since she'd been with a man for the first time?

Too long. What on earth would she say once they got upstairs?

Fortunately, once at the top of the stairs, her gaze fell on the kitchen table, and she blurted, "Um... Do you want a cookie?" She grabbed one from the cookie jar and thrust it at him. Dear Lord, he was large. He seemed to fill the room with his warmth, his presence.

He stared at her. His lips kicked up. "No."

"Are you sure?" This, she said this in a somewhat panicked tone.

He set his hand gently on her shoulder. Stroked her with his thumb. "Would you feel better if I ate one?"

Oddly enough, "Yes."

"All right then." He took a bite of the cookie, right out of her hand. She nearly dropped the damn thing. "Are you going to have one?" he asked.

"I'm not hungry." He raised his eyebrows—no words whatsoever—but she knew what he was saying. "All right." She took one, as well, but it crumbled in her grip.

He chuckled, took the whole mess from her, and piled all the cookie pieces onto a plate. "Look, Roni, we don't have to do this. Not tonight."

Relief rushed through her, quickly followed by a ribbon of irritation. "What?"

He shrugged. "We both want this to be right. It doesn't have to be right now. Okay?"

For some reason, her shoulders relaxed, and she realized she'd been tighter than a wound-up spring. "Okay." They shared a silent smile.

"And you need to know that nothing is going to happen between us that you're not ready for. Okay?"

Why on earth did that make her want him more? Oh, she knew.

"Let's sit on the sofa and chat instead."

Something inside her pinged. "You mean, you don't want to?"

He took her hand and led her into the living room, sitting next to her on the old couch. "Honey, no matter what you may think, I always want to. With you, at least."

"You do?" Well, that made her feel a little better.

"Yes, but I want you to be ready."

Oh, she was ready. So ready. "I'm just nervous."

He chuckled. "I can tell. Okay, let's pretend we're

fifteen again. Just kids. Sitting in dad's living room late at night, I dunno, watching a movie." He yawned widely, stretched and slickly draped his arm around her shoulders.

She didn't know why she jumped. She pretended it was to grab the remote. "Well, we need a movie, don't we?" When she turned on the set, a classic Bogart movie filled the room with black-and-white images and music from the forties.

"I love this one," he said, executing the slick stretching move again as soon as she resettled. This time she didn't jump. This time she nestled in. It felt wonderful, sitting side to side with him. His body was hard where hers was soft, yet they seemed a perfect fit. And he was warm.

They watched the movie in silence for a while as a hurricane battered Key Largo, and Bogart and Edward G. Robinson drank brandy and barked at each other. And Roni relaxed.

Then, something touched her neck. Stroked. Stroked again. And then, gently, he drew soothing circles along her hairline.

She sighed. "Nice."

"Mmm." He continued to caress one side of her neck, while on the other side, his breath teased her ear. Then he stopped.

She was about to complain, but he whispered, "You okay with this?"

With *this*? She pulled back…but not too far. “Your breathing on me?”

His eyes glinted. “Oh. You don’t like that? Too bad. I was just about to nibble and see if you like that.”

“Oh.” She had to respond to his humor, she just had to. She tipped her head to the side, providing him access. “All right. Nibble away.”

His breath caught. She could feel his pulse thudding against her shoulder. “You tell me if you don’t like something. Okay?”

“Okay.” And, yes. She was breathless.

Oh, oh but then his lips touched her, there, on the tender sensitive skin at her nape, and she nearly went through the roof.

Again, he stopped immediately. His beautiful brow furrowed. “You didn’t like that?” Was that a pout?

“I did. I do. Go on. Do it again.”

“Bossy,” he muttered, but she was fairly sure he was teasing. He lowered his head again, nuzzled her, teased and tormented that spot, and then, when she was about to scream with frustration, he moved on. And on.

He kissed her like that for what seemed an eternity, and she gloried in the sensations, her closeness to him, his heat. He made his way to her mouth, and she gave it to him freely. She loved that he didn’t suffocate her, that he gave her space, that he made her come to him for more.

It was the sweetest first kiss ever, even though technically, it was their second.

And, as exciting as his kiss had been to a fifteen-year-old girl, it paled in comparison to this. Oh, the thudding heart and breathless anticipation were the same. As was his scent and the feel of his lips on hers. But this kiss went beyond any other, simply because of the care he took with her. His intention to reassure her was inherent in every touch, every look.

She was safe with him. She simply was.

When his hand moved, she stilled. He'd only set it on her hip, but her reaction was instinctive. To her vexation, he stopped moving, again. Not just the stroking of his thumb. Everything.

"You, ah, still okay?" he asked, his voice barely strained at all.

"Yes." She willed him to *get back to work*, but didn't dare say the words.

"So, you're okay if I touch you here?" He stroked her hip.

"Yes," she growled.

He eased up to her waist. "Here?"

"Mmm-hmm."

"How about here?"

Dear God. He cupped her breast, just its curve. For some reason, her nipple hardened. Ached.

"Mmm."

"Is that a *yes*?"

"Yes. Yes. Yes—"

Oh. Good. God. The pad of his thumb scraped against that aroused nipple, sending a bolt sizzling through her body. It settled between her legs, causing a flood of sensations and desires, far beyond anything she'd ever experienced before.

"Maybe we should..."

Again, he froze, the second she spoke.

"Stop doing that!" She couldn't help it. The words just came out.

And, hell. He completely pulled away. Completely! Like, to the other side of the sofa! *Damn it!*

His brow rumpled with consternation. And maybe a little frustration. "Stop doing what? What did I do?"

"Stop stopping what you're doing every time I move."

"I'm not."

"You are."

His expression was repentant. "Only when I think I'm moving too fast. I don't want to scare you, and I really don't want to hurt you."

That gave her pause. She didn't want this to be scary, either. Mostly, she didn't want to be afraid of him. "What if I need you to stop? Can you stop?"

Understanding crept into his gaze. "Yes, Roni. I can. We *will*."

She could tell he meant every word, and yet, a hint of apprehension gnawed at her. "How can you be sure?"

He set his forehead on hers, kissed her nose and stared into her eyes. The scent of his breath enrobed her. He took her hand and placed it against his thudding heart. “I promise you, nothing will happen tonight that you don’t want.”

Her heart warmed. His words, his expression, the energy pouring from him, all honest and true. He seemed utterly at peace with his decision, which put her even more at ease with hers.

A smile crawled across her face, so wide and full, it made her muscles ache. She held out her arms and wrapped them around the man she knew she could trust. “Then kiss me, Mark.” And he did. But their mouths were full of laughter.

When the embrace ended, they stared at each other for a second, and then he kissed her nose and said, “Maybe we should…what?”

“What?”

“Earlier, you said, ‘Maybe we should…’ dot, dot, dot.”

“Oh.” Heat rushed to her cheeks. “I was going to say, maybe we should go into the bedroom.”

“Okay.” It was comical how quickly he leaped up.

After they kissed their way down the hall to her room—and she was more than ready to continue this adventure—he pulled away from her and started flipping through his wallet. And then he cursed.

“What’s wrong?” she asked.

He blew out a breath. “Damn it. I don’t have a condom.”

She stepped into his arms, tossed his wallet onto the floor and pulled him close to her, glorying in the hardness of his erection surging against her belly. “You don’t have to worry about getting me pregnant,” she whispered.

“You got that covered?” he asked on a pant.

She nodded but then a thought occurred. “You don’t have any STIs, do you?”

“I’ve been tested. All negative.”

“Me, too.” She went up on her tiptoes and kissed him and it was sweet. Still, he resisted.

When she frowned at him, he cleared his throat and said, “So are we, ahem, good to go?”

“I think so.” She pulled him closer, and in response, he walked her to the bed.

“Remember, tell me if you need me to stop,” he said as he lay down beside her and she began to explore his body.

“Okay,” she said. But she didn’t. Not once.

His body was glorious. So perfect, she barely noticed that, while she was undressing him, he was undressing her. When his fingertips found the scars on her shoulder and back—the reminders of the trauma that had broken her, the scars she was always so careful to cover up—he didn’t say anything, but she felt him tense.

Her gut clenched. How would he respond? Would they repulse him?

Her breath caught when he eased her to her side, when he looked at her, when he touched her there, on that mass of spidery scars.

She flinched as he bent over to see them more clearly, but that wasn't his intent.

Tears burned in her eyes as she realized what it was, his intent. When the velvet touch of his lips bathed those ugly parts of her with kisses. He kissed them in a slow, reverent journey over her shoulder and down her arm, where the worst ones were. She loved it so much—his gentleness, his care—that she decided not to be bothered by the fact that those ugly marks were bared. She didn't need to hide anything from this man. He accepted all of her. Which was, in itself, seductive.

Such seduction made it difficult for her to focus on her part in all of this, and before long, she had abdicated her study of his glorious abs and hard, muscled buttocks because the pleasure he inflicted on her body evicted every rational thought. She acquiesced to the pleasure and delight of his touch, certain it couldn't get any better than this.

And then, he slid his fingers beneath the elastic of her underwear and eased his way into the warm, wet nest between her thighs. She gasped in surprise. He caught and held her gaze as he did so, so she felt it, with what seemed like all her senses, when he touched her.

Such bliss.

She couldn't hold back a moan.

Which, apparently, had been what he was waiting for, because the moment he heard it, he repositioned himself, yanked down her panties, exposed her core with his thumbs and grinned at her before he lowered his head.

That expression was a sight she was sure would be emblazoned on her mind's eye until the day she died. Those eyes, filled with wicked intent. That smile, crooked and dimpled. The scruff of day beard that gave him the look of a dashing pirate.

And, yeah. Even that thought evaporated when his warm mouth engulfed her. She might have screamed, the pleasure was so exquisite. Whatever he was doing transported her completely. She threw back her head, sank her desperate fingers into the flesh of his shoulders, arched her back and simply *was*. She hovered in a state of glory for as long as he cared to torment her.

Her climax, when it came, was unexpected. Roni was hardly a virgin in the orgasm department but, in simple fact, there was a certain transcendent element to making love with Mark that simply had never existed for her before.

Mark collapsed on the bed and stared over at Roni, glorious in a sheen of sweat.

That had been amazing. Watching her, hearing her, bringing her to pleasure. This remarkable woman had given him the greatest gift of his life. Her trust. He was so grateful that he'd been able to honor that.

With a groan, he shifted up beside her and pulled her into his arms, loving the scent of her in the afterglow. "You okay?" he asked into her forehead.

Her response was a low, throaty laugh.

He held her and let her recover, even though he was dying. His body was still hard as a rock. His heart thudded. Every muscle was tight and aching. Even the taste of her breath made him twinge with anticipation.

She murmured something and rolled closer into his embrace.

"Good?" he asked.

"Oh, Mark," she said, her eyes damp. "That was wonderful."

He reached up and caught a tear. "Are you crying?"

"Oh, no. Yes. I don't know."

She cuddled too close to the wrong place and he groaned in agony. All he wanted to do was sink into her.

"What's wrong?" she asked, with genuine innocence, damn it all to hell, anyway. And then, she glanced down. "Oh," she said. She reached out—his pulse pounded. Then she froze, just a millimeter away, and looked at him. He nodded, gritting his teeth, knowing he was in for some sweet torture. And, God, he was so right.

Because it was. Torture. Each stroke was sure, he thought, meant to drive him right out of his mind. When she went to peel back his briefs, she stopped and glanced up at him.

"Are you okay with this?" she asked.

He nodded, because there was something in his throat that blocked everything, even his breath.

Oh, but he was. He was definitely okay with it. Especially when she lowered her head and took him into her mouth. She did it slowly, lavishly, as though reveling in him. Every atom of his being rose to meet her. It was, in a word, exquisite. A divine torture. But he could not bear it for long. He wanted—needed—more.

Gently, he pulled her up and kissed her as he rolled her onto her back and settled himself between her legs. Though he ached beyond words to take her then and there, to drive right in, he waited until she met his gaze. "Are you ready?" he asked in a whisper.

She nodded. Her eyes glimmered in the moonlight. "Yes. Yes. Please." The words melted into a moan as he fisted himself and eased in.

Ah. God. The pleasure, the feel of her, nearly blinded him. *Slowly*, he reminded himself. *Slowly.* He sucked in a deep breath, and began to move. But, in truth, they moved as one. His thrusts were long and slow, easing in and glorying in the full length of her sheath, teasing and touching every part of her that he could reach. She moaned and writhed and clutched at his skin as she wrestled against him. They both tried hard to hold back.

Tension rose to excruciating heights. Agonizing need swelled, grew and eventually exploded in an exquisite flood of mind-bending pleasure.

His release left Mark exhausted and sated and completely suffused with a strange and alluring emotion. Something from a place deep in his soul. As he pulled Roni close and kissed her brow, he realized that this noncommittal commitment might well be the most dangerous vow he'd ever made.

Chapter Seven

Roni woke in a warm nest, snuggled up against something that was even warmer. She knew, even without opening her eyes, that the arm around her, holding her close, was Mark's. His scent, his essence, enrobed her. She nuzzled deeper and his hold tightened.

God, this was bliss. She'd made the right decision, hadn't she? Fear be damned. This was worth it. This moment was worth—

She caught sight of her alarm clock and shot up with a gasp, and then gasped again when she realized she was naked. It was pointless to do so, but she yanked up the duvet to cover her chest.

Mark shot up beside her, concern rumpling his brow. "What's wrong?"

"Look how late it is!" She raked back her hair, which seemed to be everywhere.

He pulled her into his arms. "It's not that late."

Roni blew out a breath. "Gram will think that I completely forgot about her. I'm an awful granddaughter."

"Not at all." Mark rubbed her back in an attempt to soothe her. It nearly worked. "You had, ahem, other things on your mind. Besides, we did get back kind of late."

She couldn't help a spurt of laughter, though it was probably born of chagrin rather than any real humor. "Is that your story?"

"It is. And I'm sticking to it." He winked.

"Well, okay then." She pulled the duvet with her as she rounded the room, hunting for her clothes, but all she succeeded in doing was baring him. And, heavens, he was beautiful. Lean and tanned and lazing on her bed. Her gaze snagged on his sculpted chest. And his defined abs. And his…

She gasped as his, ahem, admiration for her grew.

He chuckled at her expression. "Come back to bed."

"They'll be watching for us."

"It's still early."

She did as he asked, but her thoughts were in a whirl because it hit her—oh, dear Lord—*they all knew*. Or at least Sam knew they'd spent the night together. Why hadn't she thought about that when she was so busy propositioning Mark? Heat rose on her cheeks.

"Come here," he said, and when she did, he tipped up her chin so he could look at her face. "You're beautiful in the morning."

She grimaced, and was about to correct him, but

he refused to let her. He set a finger over her lips. "You. Are. Beautiful. Always." And then, he replaced the finger with his mouth, drawing her into a drugging kiss that neither of them felt compelled to end.

They made love slowly, that morning, in the breaking sunlight, with nothing between them, nothing hidden. Again, he slowly traced each of her scars with a gentle finger, and kissed each wound, as though he could heal her from the outside in. It was even more beautiful and raw than the night before, which had seemed impossible only a few hours before.

When they were sated—for the moment—they curled up together and fell asleep again. It was midday when they roused, and the only reason Roni got up was because Mark tempted her with coffee and a muffin. After they ate and dressed, they hopped into his truck to head back to the ranch.

As he pulled out of the parking spot in front of her shop, she sighed as she took in the new facade. "I love that sign Luke made." It was beautiful, hand-painted and said, Gram's Book & Bakery in large colorful letters.

"He's a pretty good carpenter," Mark said.

"And painter," she added.

"I think maybe he missed his calling."

"He can do anything," she murmured on a sigh.

"Maybe not anything." Because he grumbled this, she chuckled.

"Your brother certainly has his skill sets," she said. "But, then again, so do you." And then, when he flushed, she kissed his cheek.

"Uh, you better stop that. I'm trying to drive here."

"Oh?" She loved his playful tone. "Are you having a hard time concentrating?" Knowing her touch aroused him made her feel daring so she slipped her hand up his thigh. She loved that he jumped.

"Hey, hon." He took her hand and held it firmly. "Don't start something you can't finish."

"I never start things I can't finish." This, she whispered against his neck.

She was stunned when he swerved to the side of the road, took off his seat belt and stared at her meaningfully. "Well?" he asked, opening his arms when she didn't move.

"Mark, we're still in town."

"So?"

"People will see."

"So?" And then, when she still didn't move into his arms, he kissed her on the nose. "Chicken."

She crossed her arms and blew out a breath. "I am definitely prepared to finish this. Just not on Main Street."

He chuckled, rebuckled his seat belt and put the truck in gear.

His blasé attitude annoyed her a little. All she'd thought about today was him. The way he felt, the way he smelled, the sensation of his body over hers, *in* hers. But he was so nonchalant about it. About everything. He'd agreed to her friends-with-benefits proposal with hardly any resistance. She wasn't sure what that meant, but for some reason, now it made her uneasy. Though she would rather die than ask him how he really felt, she couldn't stop herself as she asked, "Did you like it?"

He took his eyes off the road long enough to glance at her. "Like what?"

Like what? What else was there, but the night they'd shared? "You know." She glared at him, but he didn't notice because he was navigating the turn onto the ranch road. "Last night?"

He barked a laugh, which she didn't appreciate. "Did I like it? Roni, I loved it. Every second."

Relief gushed through her. "So you want to do it again?"

"Right now? Yes."

Oh, my. The heat in his eyes engendered a like response in her belly. "R-right now?" Nearly a stutter. Oh, right now would be lovely. She'd been fantasizing about it since before they left the bed.

He pulled the truck to a stop next to one of the cabins just north of the bunkhouse. It was surrounded by chicken-wire fencing, which was suddenly flooded with all manner of barking dogs the moment they recognized the sound of his truck. He turned off the engine and turned to her, leaning on the steering wheel. “Wanna come in and meet the current beasties?”

“You sure there’s time?”

He arched an eyebrow. “Time?”

“Before Sam comes over? Or Luke? Or DJ?”

“Or Danny? Or Lizzie? Or Emma?” He chuckled. “We’ll lock the door. They’ll have to crawl through the doggy door to get in.”

They got out of the truck and walked across the yard to his house, holding hands and wading through the puppers. With a swift and clever move, he pulled her inside and locked the door, leaving the dogs outside.

“This,” he said, throwing his arms wide, “is my place.”

She looked around, trying to take in everything. It was a comfortable bachelor pad, there was no doubt about that. An overstuffed sofa against the wall faced a large-screen TV, while a well-used table in the kitchenette was surrounded by mismatched chairs. A series of dog beds—all shapes and sizes—sat against one wall and water and food bowls lined the other. She loved that it was so… Mark.

“Well?” He stared at her with a hopeful expression.

She was spared answering when the pups pushed through the doggy door in an impatient yapping surge of canines of all shapes and sizes. When the hound dog got stuck, the Chihuahua just wormed its way around her and the beagle pushed in from underneath.

Then they all rushed her. Roni took a step back in the face of this assault. Fortunately, they all just wanted to lick her—to smell her, in some cases.

Mark chuckled. "Okay. Okay. Down. Everybody down. Sit." Unbelievably, they all sat immediately and turned their attention to Mark, all except the hound dog, who was still stuck in the doggy door. "Come on, Tallulah Belle." He was gentle as he helped her through.

She waddled over to Roni, sat and issued one long "arrorh," in welcome.

"So," he said as he started handing out treats to the drooling velociraptors tracking his every move. "What do you think?"

"Um, how many dogs do you have?"

He had to think on it. "Six right now." He bent down to ruffle the beagle's furry head. Now that he wasn't skittering among the others, Roni realized that the poor sweet thing was missing one of his front legs.

Of course, she had to go down on her knees and pat him on the head. He immediately flopped over on his back with his legs up and a beseeching expression on his fuzzy face. "Poor guy. What happened to him?"

Mark shook his head and sat on the sofa. "We never know what happened to the puppers we get. But I tell you what, he can sure get around when he wants to."

When Roni went to sit next to Mark, she saw what he meant. Snoopy was up off the floor in a flash and onto her lap the second she made one. Again, he flopped onto his back and stared up at her with big eyes. "What does he want?" she asked.

Mark gaped at her. "Have you never had a dog?"

"Of course not. I was an army brat. We moved all the time." When he stared at her, she shot him a look. "If you move overseas, sometimes your dogs have to be in quarantine for up to six months. That's not really fair to them." At least, that's what Dad had said.

"Ah." For some reason, he kissed her on the forehead. "Well, he wants you to scratch his belly. But be careful."

Her hand froze halfway there. "Why?"

Mark snickered. "Because he won't let you stop."

And indeed, after a couple of scratches on Snoopy's velvety soft tummy, she tried to pull away and he patted her hand with his front paw until she started scratching again. She just had to, he was so sweet. But the other dogs were sweet, too, and they all crowded around her for attention, as well. And some of them drooled.

Someone knocked on the door and Mark frowned at it. "I thought you locked that," Roni said with a grin.

"Yeah. I thought there might be a reason to." But there was humor in his tone. Apparently they had both accepted the fact that a repeat of last night, and this morning, would have to wait.

Their visitor turned out to be Emma, who turned to Roni with a sigh. "You're finally here. I waited and waited for you."

"Did you?" Roni smiled at her. "We had work to do for the bakery."

Emma licked her lips. "Did you bring anything?"

"Emma Jean Diem!" Lizzie pushed in behind her daughter. Danny was right behind her. "I told you to wait for me. And you should never ask for treats." She shot Roni a repentant smile.

"But did you? Bring anything?" Danny asked with a grin. Lizzie glowered at him.

"Sorry." Roni tried to remove Snoopy from her lap, but he wouldn't budge. How could a beagle that small weigh so much? "I didn't get any baking done this morning."

Emma put her hands on her hips. "Well, what were you doing instead?"

Uhhh...

Thankfully, Mark leaped in to rescue her. "There's lots to do to get a bakery ready," he said. Roni flushed when, for some reason, Danny and Lizzie exchanged a glance.

But Emma wasn't impressed. She tipped her head

to the side and sighed. “Oh, bother,” she said in a credible impression of Pooh.

“I’ll do some baking tomorrow. I promise.”

A little pout came out. “But what if I don’t see you tomorrow?”

“We’ll go into town,” her mother said.

Danny nodded. There was a wicked twist to his lips. “I’m sure Roni will appreciate all the help she can get on opening day.”

“Ooh, are you nervous?” Lizzie sat next to Roni on the couch and when Snoopy nudged her hand, she scratched his neck. Now he had two masseuses. He let out a soft little groan that Roni could only interpret as bliss. Well. After all he’d been through, the little guy deserved some TLC, didn’t he?

“Roni?” Emma asked. “Are you nervous about opening day?”

“I’m very excited.” It was true. Whenever she thought of it, having her own bakery, her heart trilled.

“But what if no one comes?” Leave it to Emma to voice her own worst fears.

Mark jumped in with a hearty pirate laugh. “More for us, my girlie. More for us.” Then he tickled her until she squealed.

“Oh, that reminds me. Emma, I got you something at the market. It’s in the truck. Mark, do you mind?” Roni gestured to her lap. There was no way she was getting up.

"Sure."

Mark headed outside and Emma followed chanting, "What is it? What is it? What is it?"

When they were gone, Lizzie shook her head. "You didn't have to do that."

"I wanted to. It's just a backpack, for when she starts school."

"She'll be thrilled," Danny said. He sat in one of the dining room chairs and the miniature pinscher hopped on his lap. The larger dogs crowded around, as if awaiting their turns. "She loves things to put her things in." He winked. "Just like her mother."

"Don't start with me and my purses," Lizzie warned him. But nobody was starting with anything, because a shrill scream of excitement came from outside.

Emma ran in, her face aglow, clutching her new backpack. She yelled, "I love it, I love it, I love it. Thank you, Roni."

"You're welcome, sweetie." Roni smiled at her. "Remember, you can always ask me anything you want about school, anytime."

They talked for a while about school and rules and Emma's growing excitement to start, and all the while, Roni rubbed Snoopy's belly. It was funny, how soothing that was, she thought. He really was an adorable creature with those big brown eyes and soft ears. When he finally stirred, and left her lap, she missed his weight.

"Are you going to take one of the puppies?" Emma asked after a bit. And then, before Roni could answer, she said, "Which dog do you want? You can't have Daisy 'cuz she's mine." She stood between Roni and Daisy, just in case.

"Oh, honey, I would never take your dog. And I couldn't take a puppy home without Gram agreeing to it. A dog is a lot of responsibility."

"Which you will learn, once the doctor says it's okay to have one." Lizzie glanced at Roni. "We're looking at December."

"How wonderful." Mark had explained that once Emma got final clearance, she'd be able to play with all the animals, which, judging from the way Emma was eyeing the pups, couldn't be soon enough.

She toyed with the strap of her new backpack. "Your gram told me she wanted a puppy."

"Did she?"

Emma nodded. "We talked about it yesterday. She had a dog when she was a little girl, you know."

"I did not know that."

"She *really* wants one." Emma batted her lashes.

"Well," Mark said, saving Roni once again, "You're welcome to take one home for a trial run. It's really important that adoption is a good fit for everyone, don't you think?"

The suggestion made Roni feel better, because in her heart of hearts, she had always wanted a pet.

When she'd been with Anthony, bringing an innocent animal into the house had been unthinkable.

As though to seal the deal, Snoopy jumped back onto the sofa, and into her lap. Though everyone laughed, to Roni, it was a sign. She agreed to take the pooch on a strictly probationary basis because she had to make sure having a dog wouldn't be a problem for Gram.

It turned out to be a silly worry. Gram fell in love immediately. So, apparently, did Snoopy. He curled up in the older woman's lap and stayed there all the way home.

Mark was riding on a high as he watched Roni and Milly—and Snoopy—drive away. Part of it was his blossoming relationship with Roni, and memories of their lovemaking and how happy it made him to be closer to her, but it was more than just that. Watching her with his dogs had really hit him hard…in a good way.

It was tough for him to imagine anyone growing up without a pet to love, and it had been pretty clear that she wasn't comfortable at first, but it hadn't taken long for her to warm up to them. Even the drooling. In fact, she might, in time, become as fanatical about the pups as he was. No one could fake the delight in their laughter when all the dogs, well, dog-piled on her with kisses.

He was distracted, his mind full of cheerful

thoughts, as he turned from the drive and followed Danny and his family back into the big house, so he didn't expect a hand to reach out and grab his arm as he passed DJ's office. Naturally, he started, but then relaxed when he realized it was Sam.

"Good morning," he said.

She frowned. "Good afternoon." And then she added, "Get in here."

It was Mark's turn to frown. "Get in here… please?"

"Please." A growl.

Mark had no idea why Sam was annoyed with him, but he knew her well enough to comply, so he stepped inside the office and closed the door. He suppressed the shiver that hit him every time he was in this room. Before it had been DJ's office, it had belonged to his grandfather, and still had the same old oppressive air. Back then, the only occasions Mark had been hauled in here were the times he'd been in trouble. He'd never felt comfortable in this room.

"What is it, Sam?" he asked, though he had an inkling. She wanted the scoop. Sam always wanted the scoop.

"What happened last night?"

He gazed at her with innocent eyes. "We texted you. Remember? It took longer than we thought to get everything done."

"So you slept over?"

"Mmm-hmm." He averted his gaze.

She rolled her eyes. "I think we both know what's going on."

He bit back a grin. "Do we?"

"I see the way you look at her. I see the way she looks at you. Are you and Roni a thing?"

"She looks at me?"

"Don't avoid the question."

"How does she look at me?"

"Really?" Sam made a growling noise when she realized she wouldn't get him to answer her. "All right, fine. She gets all googly-eyed."

He couldn't hold back his grin. "Really?"

"Yes. Really. Now spill."

"There's nothing to spill. Roni and I are just friends..."

"Friends who have *sleepovers*?" He didn't respond, so she took another tack. "I deserve to know what's happening because I'm the one who set you two up."

"Well, thank you for that," Mark set his hands on his hips. "But what happens between the two of us is private."

Sam blew out a breath. "Oh, right. All of a sudden Mark Stirling doesn't kiss and tell?"

"When have I ever told?"

"That's not the point."

"Is there a point?"

His sister blew something else out. It might have

been a bad word. “Yes. You don’t know about everything Roni’s been through. You can’t just treat her like all your other women.”

“I don’t have any other women.”

He probably shouldn’t have said anything because Sam jumped on that like a duck on a june bug. “Aha! So you admit it.”

“Admit what?”

“You said you don’t have any *other* women. Which infers you *have* Roni.”

Irritation prickled on his nape. “Sam. This is none of your business.” And, when his sister opened her mouth to rebut, he held up *the hand*. “Not. Your. Business.”

“I’m your sister. I worry about you.”

“Me?”

Her expression turned solemn, which rarely happened. “You know you’re getting more involved with Roni…”

“Mmm-hmm.”

She looked hesitant, for a change. “But there are things about her you don’t know.”

He doubted that, but forced a smile. “Whatever that may be, don’t you think I should hear it from her?”

“But, Mark. What if she…hurts you?”

A harsh laugh bubbled up. “If you were so all fired worried about me, why did you set us up in the first place?” When she didn’t respond, he continued.

"You can't feel responsible for whatever happens between us from now until eternity because at one point, you invited both of us to lunch at the same time." He was trying to illustrate how ridiculous such a prospect was, but she didn't get it.

"I can't help it."

"Sam. Relax. Roni's the only one who knows the details of what she's been through. I can't blame her for setting limits if she needs them."

"What do you mean...*limits*?"

"Hmm?"

"What kind of limits did she set?" And then, when he didn't answer, she said, "Mark. Someone is going to get hurt here. I just don't see how this isn't going to end in disaster."

"Like what?"

"She'll want more?"

He barked a laugh. *Good.*

"You'll want more?"

He swallowed the laugh and it caught in his throat. Maybe he already did want more. Picket fence. Babies. The whole deal. Everything.

She stared at him, taking in his telling expression. "Oh, no."

Oh, yes. "Sam, I want that woman in my life, however I can have her."

She lurched back as though his words had burned her. "You sound like you're in love with her."

Love? Where on earth had Sam come up with

that idea? He wasn't yet sure how he felt about Roni, but love was a little extreme considering how long they'd been an item—if you could even call it that. Wasn't it?

Sam gaped at him. "Oh, hell. You are, aren't you?"

He raked his hair, sighed heavily. "Sam, just quit, okay? We're…happy. With whatever this is, now. Can't you just be happy for us, too?"

"What if she never changes her mind? What if she never wants to get married? Like ever?"

Mark shrugged. "Then we'll be old friends together."

"But don't you want kids? You've always loved kids."

His shoulders slumped. "I suppose we'll deal with that as it comes."

Sam shook her head. "Mark, I love Roni. I do. But I think you're setting yourself up for a broken heart."

"It's not going to end that way," he said in a tone intended to close the discussion. And it did. But it couldn't keep him from wondering whether he really knew what he was talking about after all.

Roni thought she was prepared for opening day, but she wasn't. When she came downstairs early, just because she was so excited, there was already a line outside. Granted, Gwen, Tiffy and Charlie were just there to make sure she had some customers—which was so sweet—but they still walked away with a bag of breakfast pastries. Gwen offered to stay and help when she saw more people lining up, but Roni politely demurred because, frankly, she was too busy to also keep an eye on a pair of almost-three-year-olds. "Come back this evening," she suggested. "We can chat." She turned to the twins. "And I'll introduce you all to Snoopy."

The twins hooted with joy, and quickly got hustled out by their mother. But Roni had little time to reflect on the matter, because the next customer—a middle-aged cowboy with a full mustache and a hungry look in his eye—stepped up. Gram, who'd come downstairs and taken a seat at one of the little tables, greeted him with a chipper "Howdy, Merle." Roni didn't know why she was surprised; she should have suspected that Gram would know just about everyone in town. Thank heaven she was there, because a steady stream of future regulars continued like that for several hours. In addition to the newbies, DJ and Sam came by with Dorthea, then Crystal, then Lizzie and Danny. It was practically a party when they all crowded around Gram and ate their treats.

At one point while they were there, a woman walked through the door and, for a second, all conversation stopped. Just…stopped. She was a beautiful woman, whoever she was—no doubt she stopped conversations often, just walking through a door—but she clearly did not belong in a humble bakery in this humble town. Roni wasn't the fancy type, but she knew a Gucci purse and couture dress when she saw them. And the skin of this misdirected socialite was so flawless, Roni was certain she must have it vacuumed every morning.

She stepped up to the front of the line—the gentlemen waiting let her—and took in Roni. From head to apron. A tiny line lifted on her forehead, then she turned her attention to the display case. Her nose twitched several times and then, in a soft, well-modulated tone, she ordered a small black coffee, took it and paid without so much as a thank-you, and then swept from the premises. As she walked down the street toward a red Corvette, she dropped the cup and its contents into a trash can. Roni only noticed because she was watching. Then the woman turned around and glanced back. When her smile unfolded, it sent a shiver down Roni's back.

"Who the heck was that?" she asked Sam when she came to the counter to refill Gram's teacup.

"Don't worry about her," Sam said, waving a hand. "That's just Sophia."

She looked like a Sophia. "How do you think she gets her hair into a swirl like that?"

Sam shrugged. "Lacquer?"

"She threw her coffee away. She didn't even drink it."

"That's because she only stopped by to look at you."

"Me?" A squeak. "Why?"

"Can't you guess? She used to date Mark."

Roni's eyebrows shot up. Her body heated. Her fingers curled. "That woman? That woman dated Mark?" It was hard to hold back a sharp laugh. Those two were about as opposite as two people could get.

"They didn't date for long. It was never going to work, anyway, because Sophia wanted to remake him in her image. I think she imagined they'd be the reigning king and queen of Butterscotch Ridge or something." Sam sighed. "She never really got over him."

"That's sad."

"Yeah. I'm real broken up about it." Sam was deadpan, but Roni knew better. "She could have been my *sister in-law*." She shuddered.

"Yeah, but just think. You could have been a princess…or something."

Sam snorted. "Or something. Yeah."

Shortly after that, there was another surge and the Stirlings left to make room for new customers, promising to come back again soon. Thank the good Lord Roni had baked extra items and frozen them, because the goodies she had on display were gone before noon. At one point, she had the brilliant idea of taking orders for tomorrow—everything from fresh bread to cakes to ginger cookies. She tried not to panic as she saw the box of orders filling up.

Had she really worried there might not be a need for a bakery in this town?

Ye gods.

Her heart leaped when Mark walked through the door. He gave her a quick kiss and asked what he could do to help. Because Gram was chatting and laughing with a circle of friends on the bookstore side, Roni immediately set him to work clearing the tables and tidying up, and when that was done, he refilled the display case for her while she manned the front counter. It was great having another set of hands, but, honestly, Mark was much more than that. He would walk past and murmur little encouragements as she worked. He even flirted with Gram's friends until they dissolved into octogenarian titters. But, hey, a hot guy was a hot guy no matter how old you were.

And, yes, Roni made sure to tease him about his new entourage.

The crowd petered out at around 4:00 p.m., which, she decided, was closing time. "Thanks for being here," she said to both Gram and Mark as she turned the sign and closed the door. "You were both great help."

Gram snagged the last molasses cookie, one Roni had been saving for her. "That was fun," she said. "I can't remember when I've had so much fun. But now I need a nap."

"It was the opening, Gram. It probably won't be this busy every day."

Gram sent her a grin. "We'll see. Mark, you should stay for supper, since you were so much help."

"Why, thank you, Milly."

Her smile widened. "Wonderful. I can't wait to see what you make." And before he could respond, she went upstairs. Apparently, she didn't close the upper door, because Snoopy immediately came tearing down the stairs in a manic series of clickity-clacks. Oh, not to see Roni or Mark, or anything that would show his devotion to them. He came to smell what he missed. Apparently, the scents were fascinating.

Mark laughed and pulled Roni into his arms. "I am so proud of you," he said. "You did great. I knew you would."

Roni gazed up into his eyes and sniffed a little. "I'm proud, too." She set her palm on his cheek. "Mark, I'm so happy. Thank you for…everything."

"I didn't do much."

"You did more than you know." She glanced at the box of orders and sighed. "Although I think I'm going to need more help."

Mark chuckled. "I agree, but don't look at me. DJ's a little sore that I ducked out this afternoon. They're moving one of the herds over to the lake because the stream dried up."

Roni's heart clenched. "Is that a bad thing?"

"Probably." He pulled her close again and kissed her forehead. "But it happens every summer about now."

"I would hate to think I'm keeping you from your work."

"It's just for today. Besides," he said with a grin, "I wanted to be here for you."

"Aww. That's sweet." She thanked him with a kiss. "Tell DJ that you were a lot of help today. I don't know what I would have done if you hadn't been here."

He leaned against the counter and nibbled at a lemon poppy-seed muffin. "You would have managed. You always do."

"Sure," she said. "But it is so much better not to have to manage all alone." And, yeah. It hit her. She really needed to hire some help. Today had been successful only because Mark and Gram had been here to back her up. "Do you think Lizzie would be interested in a job?"

He shrugged. "She does the books for the ranch, but maybe. I'll ask her when I get home, but remember, if you hire Lizzie, you probably get Emma for free."

Roni had to smile. "I'd love that." Though it would be only afternoons for Emma now that school was starting. She would be a charming hostess.

"So what do you want to do, now that your work for the day is done?" Mark asked in a sexy voice.

Roni was pretty sure of what he had in mind, and to be honest, she wanted that, too. He was too tempting by far. It took almost everything in her to gently push him away.

"Mark, I'm a baker. I've only just begun to work for the day."

He glanced at the door and the Closed sign. "Umm..."

She chuckled and handed him the box by the register. "Here are the orders for tomorrow. Could you write them all out on one list so I know how many of each to make tonight?"

"Tonight?" A squeak.

"Mmm-hmm. Oh, and be sure to note who each order is for. I don't want to get them mixed up. While you're doing that, I'll start laminating the pastry dough."

"*Laminating* the pastry dough?" His expression was priceless. She had to laugh.

"If you're a good boy, I'll teach you all my secrets."

"Laminating the pastry dough?"

She laughed again. He was adorable. He'd be even more adorable once she got him into an apron. "It's fun. Trust me."

He blew out a breath. "All right, Veronica James. I humbly place myself in your hands."

Chapter Eight

For Mark's entire life, roles on Stirling Ranch had always been very clearly defined, according to his grandfather's preferences. Men worked the ranch, and women took care of the house. Sam was the only one who'd been able to cross the lines, and that was because she was so damn good at what she did, the old man didn't complain. But Mark had never really been able to break out of the limitations that had been set for him, because he'd never been allowed to explore what was outside those parameters. So he hadn't even really realized what he'd been missing…until now.

Now, thanks to Roni, he saw how wrong his grandfather had been.

There was so much joy in mixing batters and doughs, and watching them poof up in the oven. And, all right, he liked tasting the finished product, still warm from the baking sheet, as well. It wasn't only fun, but damn cathartic, too.

Hell—he freaking loved baking.

He had so much fun baking with Roni that Gram

came down to see what the heck the racket was… and to remind him about dinner.

He hated that they had to take a break, but he knew he needed something other than sugar in his system, and he was pretty adequate with grilled-cheese sandwiches. While he made the sandwiches, Roni whipped up a salad.

After supper, Gram went to watch the news while Mark and Roni went back to the bakery. Roni let him make cupcakes. She showed him how to cream the wet ingredients first and then add in the dry for the first batch, but when she moved on to cookies and let him handle the second batch of cupcakes himself, he forgot to change the beater on the mixer and ran it too high, so a cloud of flour erupted. It went everywhere.

It even scared Snoopy, who hightailed it to the divan, where it was safe.

But Roni just laughed. "This happens sometimes," she said, and then went on to show him where he'd gone wrong.

The thing he loved the most about baking, however, was the end result. After the cupcakes came out of the oven and had cooled, it was time to frost them using a pastry bag. Mark was nervous about this part, and the first time he tried, he did a pretty sloppy job. It hardly looked like anything that could go into the pastry case for sale.

Roni set aside his monstrosity and said, "This

one is for us," then positioned herself behind him, took hold of his hand and showed him the motion he needed. "That's good," she said, clearly lying, after his second try. He shot her a sardonic look. "All we need to work on now is the pressure." She stayed with him until he got it.

Granted, his swirls were not as clean and perfect as hers, but he still felt proud that he was at least beginning to get the hang of it...and that he was able to do something to help speed her through the pile of orders that awaited her.

He grinned at her as she carried the finished batches to the fridge. "I'm getting pretty good at this," he said as he picked up one of his cupcakes and licked the frosting. Strawberry. It was delicious.

It was bad timing, though, because Snoopy chose that moment to leap onto his lap, which somehow smooshed the frosting all over his face. Still, pretty delicious.

"Oh, no," Roni said sternly, as she ran back to the table and pulled Snoopy from Mark's lap. "That's not for doggies. Here." She handed him a different treat, which he gobbled up.

"I want one of those," Mark said.

She laughed. "It's a dog treat."

"It looks like a cookie."

"It's a dog treat. I should know. I make them special." She eyed him for a moment and her expression changed. He wasn't sure what that look was, humor or horniness. His pulse kicked up as she came closer, and closer still. "And you look…"

A shiver skittered down his spine. Heat pooled in his lap. "What?" he asked, on a bated breath. "What do I look like?"

She eased herself onto his lap. His interest…rose. She noticed and smiled, then wiggled around. "What do I look like?" His voice cracked.

"You look…delicious," she murmured, and then, she licked him.

"What did I tell you about starting something you're not prepared to finish?" he growled.

"Oh, I intend to finish," she said, leaning in, and licked him again.

She probably would have continued forever—and he would have let her—but she was distracted by Snoopy's manic barking. They both glanced at the dog, and then turned toward the stairs, the location of his distress.

Mark's mood deflated immediately. Because there was Gwen, with her arms crossed, frowning at them both.

Roni leaped from Mark's lap and smoothed down her apron. She wasn't sure why, other than she was fairly certain her cousin was annoyed.

"You asked me to come over this evening. So we could chat," she said with a stiff voice. Oh, and a glare at Mark.

"I did. I did!" Why was she so jumpy? She had every right to be kissing Mark, darn it. "Thank you for coming. Uh, Mark and I were just celebrating a very successful day."

"I see that."

Oh, dear. He still had a swathe of frosting on his cheek. She went to the sink, quickly dampened a cloth and handed it to him. "We just finished most of the prep for tomorrow, so you have perfect timing."

Mark stood and took off his apron. Roni hated to see it go, because he was really, truly cute in an apron. "I should head home, anyway," he said, a hint of apology in his tone.

"Do you have to?"

"I have a lot of work to make up for at the ranch. Plus, I've got to take care of the dogs." His smile was resigned.

She hadn't realized how much she'd been expecting that they would make love tonight, that he would stay over. She hadn't realized how much she'd wanted that. For some reason, her fingers tightened on his arm. He smiled down at her and gave her a kiss. "I'll come by tomorrow after I finish work. You call if it gets busy and I'll try to break away—"

"Actually, if it gets busy, she can call me," Gwen announced.

Mark didn't even look at her. He kept his gaze on Roni. Something about it made heat rise within her. When he leaned in again, she thought it was to give her another kiss, but he whispered in her ear. "I'll be thinking about you tonight," he said in a teasing voice, one that made her grin. Then he snagged his deformed cupcake and his Stetson, and headed out the door. He waved at her as he started his truck and then flashed her with the lights for good measure.

It was hard watching him go, but she did so with a smile on her face. Because she'd see him tomorrow. And the day after that, most likely.

She locked the front door and leaned against it with a sigh.

Gwen erupted, ruining her moment. "What the hell was that?" she bellowed, sending Snoopy into another rhapsody of howls.

"Hush, Snoopy." Roni took off her apron, folded it and set it on the counter.

"Veronica. What. The. Actual. Hell? You were kissing Mark Stirling!"

"Yes, Gwen, I was. What's the big deal?"

"Really? Really?" Her cousin rolled her eyes heavenward. "'What's the big deal?' she says. I told you to be careful with him. I told you not to get involved. Why didn't you listen to me?"

"Can we take this upstairs? I'm tired."

"Because you think I won't yell in front of Gram?"

Roni started shutting off the lights and tried to

hold on to her earlier elation. It had been a magnificent day, and the evening had been tremendous fun with Mark. Gwen and her negativity threatened to erase her happiness. But she knew better. She would not allow anyone to do that to her. Not anymore.

She forced a dazzling smile. "You need a cookie," she said as she flicked off the last light and shooed Snoopy up the stairs. She gestured for Gwen to precede her. "Come on. Let's go up."

Gwen harrumphed, but complied, though she clomped heavily on the stairs. As she pushed through the upper door into the kitchen, she grumbled, to Gram apparently, who was sipping a cup of tea, "They were kissing."

"Oh." Gram took a sip. "Good. I like that boy."

"Seriously?" Gwen asked, imploring the ceiling. "What is it about Mark Stirling that makes women lose their minds?"

"I have not lost my mind," Roni said, raiding the cookie jar for three of Gram's molasses cookies, which she plated and set on the table. Two had been co-opted before she sat.

Gwen waggled hers in Roni's direction. "You were canoodling with a guy who goes through women like toilet paper. After I warned you to steer clear."

"Mark Stirling?" Gram asked. "Didn't you date him, Gwenny?"

Gwen went red. "I didn't date him, but my best

friend Polly did, and he dumped her. Heartlessly." She whirled on Roni. "She never really got over him."

"Hmm." Gram nibbled her cookie. "Isn't Polly married to Ricky MacLean?"

"Yes."

"Don't they have five children?"

"Yes."

Gram shot Gwen a glance, then returned to her tea. "I think she got over him."

Roni scooted closer. "Is that why you have negative feelings for Mark, Gwen?" Her over-the-top reaction to a simple face-licking seemed to indicate that was the case.

"I don't have *any* feelings for Mark." Her flush deepened. "I just can't stand him."

"Those are feelings," Gram observed.

"Look, he dumped Polly. Just like he's dumped every woman in town." She turned to Roni. "I'm worried that he's going to do the same to you. And after your divorce, well, I just don't want you to get hurt."

Roni set her hand on Gwen's clenched fist. "He's not going to hurt me. I won't allow it."

Gwen's snort was vociferous. Roni handed her a much-needed tissue. "You won't *allow* it? How on earth are you going to keep that man from breaking your heart? Seriously. How are you going to be the only woman in the entire state to emerge unscathed from his evil wiles?"

Gram, now deep into her cookie, waggled her eyebrows. "Evil wiles," she murmured to herself and then chuckled as though it reminded her of something.

"He is not evil, Gwen. I wish you would stop being so negative. I really like him."

"Polly really liked him, too. Look where that got her."

"Married to a hunky rancher with five children?" Gram grinned. "Ricky is hunky."

"That is not the point."

Gram shrugged. "He is." She glanced at the clock. "Oh, dear." She quickly refilled her teacup, snagged the third cookie and hustled into the living room.

Gwen made a face. "What was that about?"

Roni smiled. "Probably time for one of her shows." And, indeed, the TV erupted with the trademark *ca-kung* of a famous show about law and order.

"Good." Gwen fixed Roni with a hard stare. "Now that we're in private, you can explain to me how you intend to elude the Mark Stirling curse."

"That is not a thing."

"It actually is. Come on, Roni. Look at the facts. Be realistic. He's a charming, fun-loving, cute-as-all-get-out man who has no intention of settling down. Ever."

"And that's why he's perfect for me."

Gwen gaped at her. "What?"

"Mark and I have an…agreement."

"Oh, no." Gwen grimaced. "What kind of agreement, exactly?"

Roni leaned in. "Well, *exactly*...it's none of your beeswax."

"Come on."

"Mark and I are just friends."

"Just friends don't make out with each other," Gwen snorted. And then, realization dawned. Her eyes widened. "Oh, my God. Friends with benefits?" She said it like it tasted bad. "Is that what you are? With Mark Stirling?"

"What was that I was just saying about beeswax?"

Gwen shook her head. "Roni. No. Women always lose in relationships like this. Guys take advantage, and then, when they've had their fun, poof, they're gone. You're setting yourself up for heartbreak."

How on earth could she make her cousin understand? She knew she had to, or every single time they saw each other the conversation would go exactly like this. For all eternity. "He's great company. I love being with him. Neither of us wants marriage. How is this a bad choice? How could spending time with him destroy me?"

"He could dump you."

Roni ignored the little jab in her chest. "He could. And I could end it with him. But we're both adults. We both know what we are doing and, frankly, we respect each other. And we trust each other." And then, when Gwen refused to be moved, she added, "Look, this is what I want. For good or bad."

"But mostly bad."

"No. Mostly good." She let her feelings shine through her smile in the hope that it would convince Gwen that she knew what she was doing, that Mark would never hurt her, that this arrangement could go on forever and ever. "I know what I'm doing. Trust me."

But all it did was make Gwen grunt something that sounded like, "Whatever. It's your funeral."

Mark was irritated with himself for leaving the bakery, even though it was obvious Roni and her cousin had issues to discuss. Although he was happy enough to escape Gwen's vitriol, he had to admit to himself that he'd hoped the night would go a little differently.

So he was irritated and regretful when he got home, and then couldn't sleep for thinking of her. Even the dogs were restless.

He thought about calling her several times, but reminded himself that they both had to get up early for work. Still, somehow, he found himself with his cell in his hand and pressing Call under her picture.

The phone rang for a bit before she picked up. "Hello?" she said.

He heard the smile in her voice. He leaned back

on the pillows and grinned up at the ceiling. "This isn't too late, is it?"

She chuckled. "I don't care. I miss you."

"I wish I hadn't left."

"I know. But it was for the best. Gwen and I needed to have a talk. She's convinced you're going to break my heart."

"I won't. I promise."

"I know. How could you? After all, we both agreed to keep this casual."

Something sizzled through him at her words, and it wasn't a good kind of sizzle. She was right. They had both agreed. But he didn't feel *casual* in the least. Not about her. Not anymore. When the heck had that happened?

"Mark?"

"Yeah. I'm here. Just thinking about you."

"Mmm." A sexy purr. "What are you wearing?"

He huffed a laugh and glanced down. "Sweat-pants?"

"Oooh. Sexy."

A full-bodied chuckle came out. "What are you wearing?"

"I shouldn't tell you."

"Why not?" God, it felt good, the warmth in his chest. Just hearing her voice made him feel good.

"As you always tell me, I shouldn't start something I can't finish."

"Right." He grinned.

"I'm wearing my Elmo pajamas. I hope you can handle that."

"That is…so hot." God, he loved her sense of humor. Her everything, maybe. "I wish I was there."

"Me, too." She was quiet for a while—they both were, and it was comfortable. "So," she said in a chipper tone. "Did you call to have phone sex?"

Had he? He wasn't sure. "Do you want to have phone sex?"

She snickered. "Not tonight."

"Do you have a headache?"

"Quit it. I would love to have phone sex with you, but I have to get up in a few hours and I should really go to sleep."

He glanced at his alarm clock. "A few hours?"

"I'm a baker, remember. I still have to box up the special orders, make the croissants and the pastries, not to mention the loaves for the customers who ordered them. Those all have to be made fresh each morning. I can't let my customers down. Not on the second day."

He winced. "I should have known. I'm sorry to bother you."

"Mark," she said with a smile. "You know you can call me anytime. About anything. Get it?"

"Got it."

"Good. Now, close your eyes and go to sleep. I will see you tomorrow. Okay?"

"Okay," he said in a whisper, and then he stayed

on the line until she hung up. He did close his eyes and he did fall asleep. And his dreams were filled with thoughts of her.

The second day, the bakery was a little quieter. While Roni was disappointed it wasn't a mad rush again, she was also a little relieved. Until school got out. Then it got busy again.

She grinned as she saw one of her favorite people coming through the door.

"Emma!" she called, rounding the counter and kneeling down to her eye level. "How was your first day at school? Tell me all about it!"

She stared at Roni, her eyes wide and her cheeks aglow. She threw out her arms and twirled. "It was fantastical."

"Was it?" Roni glanced at Lizzie, who grinned.

"My teacher is Miss Linder and we did math on a *chalkboard*, and mom packed me a lunch and I traded my banana for some chips and there are boys in my room. Boys."

"Why don't you keep me company at the counter and tell me everything?"

She had more to say, so Lizzie set her up on a stool with an éclair and Emma talked as Roni helped customers.

As promised, Mark came by when he finished work at the ranch, and because Roni had been able to finish most of the prep for the next day in between the rushes—and because she had so much repounded butter—there was no need to conscript him to help that evening. As a result, they spent a lovely evening chatting and watching TV with Gram. And then, when Gram went to bed…they did, too. It was extra exciting because they had to be *really* quiet.

As the days passed, Roni began to feel the rhythm of her business and the community she served. She got better at guessing how much she needed to make each day and got really good at making—and selling—frozen pies, banana breads and cookies. Aussie Bites—with quinoa, thank you very much—were customer favorites. Even Mark liked them. So she didn't mention they were healthy in any way.

The fact was, business was just way too good. Not a bad problem to have, but still, the only time she got to see Mark was when he came over in the evenings.

He came by almost every day after working on the ranch. Some days he'd come in all dirty and she'd make him go up and take a shower. Sometimes he spent the night. Sometimes he didn't.

Gram loved the busyness in the shop. She held court like a Grande Dame. Although there were definitely more customers in the store than before, they sold a lot more baked goods than books—which certainly made Gram happy. In response, Roni ordered all kinds of magazines, and left them scattered around on the tables for her customers to read. It wasn't long before people started coming in for a cup of coffee and a pastry and staying for hours.

Gram especially loved lounging on the divan near her books with Snoopy on her lap. Those two had quickly become fast friends. Now that he'd been around for a while, Roni couldn't imagine life without him. Somehow he knew not to bark at strangers in the store, but upstairs, in their apartment, he was like a rottweiler if he heard so much as a creak on the stairs.

To Roni's surprise, the B&G was one of her biggest customers. They wanted fresh cakes and pies to fill out their dessert menu. The owner, Chase McGruder, also asked if she could take on his bread order, but she had to ask him to come back to her once she had help.

While Lizzie said she didn't have the capacity to help—with the pregnancy and all—Maria, the housekeeper at the ranch, had a brother who was looking for work. Roni was nervous interviewing Carlos—she'd never interviewed anyone for a job before—but she liked him. He was tall and strong and seemed capable of working with both the heavier bread doughs and some of the more delicate pastries. He'd worked in a bakery before and was willing to work the crazy hours and learn the recipes. His wife, Lupe, had baking experience, too. They seemed like a perfect fit, so Roni hired them both.

For her part, she had no experience running a business with employees, and dealing with the paperwork involved. The thought of workman's compensation and 1099s made her brain hurt. Fortunately, Lizzie was on top of it all and helped her through it.

Somehow, instead of stress, Roni felt excited and powerful. This was a thing that belonged to her. She'd built it—sure, with help—and had turned her vague idea into a full-fledged business. And she loved the work. Every second.

It wasn't all work, though. There was a lot of play. Sunday suppers at the Stirling Ranch became a staple. Mark made it a point to take Roni into the Tri-Cities every so often for a movie or a trip to Costco. And, of course, when Lizzie and Danny wanted some time alone, Roni happily volunteered to watch Emma.

She loved those days. She especially enjoyed tea time, where Gram and Emma sipped on chamomile and nibbled on whatever goodies were on offer. Soon, other little girls—and a few boys—started coming over on Saturday afternoons with big round eyes and hopeful looks. It wasn't long until Saturday afternoon Story Hour was an actual thing. It thrilled Roni, because the events were the perfect marriage of her two favorite things: baking and kiddos. The children would arrive to find the shop closed for their very own exclusive "tea party" and reading of whatever storybook they'd selected by show of hands the week before. Slowly but surely, she got to know most of the children in town.

One of her favorites was Jack, Crystal's son. He was endearing and smart, though she'd heard from his mother that some people around town—Mrs. Anders, the school principal, included—seemed to think he had behavioral issues. But Roni knew better. She'd seen children like Jack before. He didn't process information the way others did, so he was frustrated when he didn't succeed as quickly. And when he became frustrated, like many other children with challenges like ADD and dyslexia, he needed a little extra encouragement.

Because they lived so close to each other—practically next door, as Roni lived over the bookstore and Crystal and Jack lived over the B&G—they became fast friends. It seemed natural for Crystal to watch Gram, or for Roni to take care of Jack after school, when Crystal had to work. And she really did work hard.

"So you really have two jobs," Roni said one night over wine when Crystal came by to pick up her son. She hadn't been working at the B&G that night. She'd been down in the Tri-Cities visiting a client who was undergoing chemotherapy, and had hired Crystal to help with pain and nausea.

"I do," Crystal said. "But the aromatherapy and massage are more of a passion."

"There can't be much of a clientele here in town."

Crystal's eyes lit up. "That's why I'm working on setting up a website for my lotions and soaps. I make them in my kitchen. I figure if I can get this online business to take off, Jack and I won't have to worry about money as much."

Roni nodded. It must be hard to be a single mother, she thought. "You should talk to Lizzie. She's been amazing helping me figure out the business side of a bakery."

Crystal nodded. "Good idea. Lizzie's great. Heck, all the Stirlings are. They've been so supportive since my husband was killed." Brandon had been a Marine, stationed overseas, when he'd been killed by an IED. Apparently, he and Luke had been friends, stationed together—but Luke never talked about it. He never talked about a lot of stuff, which Roni understood more than she would have liked. Sam called him a hermit, but Roni saw him a lot, because he lived nearby. And he had a sweet tooth.

When she thought about it, she had to admit that a great deal of her happiness was due to the Stirlings, the family that had surrounded her, and embraced her, and supported her. And the man who made her body heat with passion, who made her feel safe and protected in his arms, in his bed, without demanding anything in return.

Mark had been exactly what she'd needed. He'd been gentle and patient and cognizant of her needs, he'd moved at her pace, which must have been frustrating for him. He'd helped her regain her confidence as a woman. As a person.

He made her happy.

She had to ignore the hovering thought that at some point he might decide he wanted more in his life…maybe even children. And when that happened she'd have to tell him the truth. And then, of course, he'd end whatever this was between them.

It was probably best, for the moment, to just ignore reality, and enjoy what they had while it lasted. There was always tomorrow for heartbreak.

As they got further into autumn, Roni and Mark eased into a comfortable routine, despite his misgivings. Which he kept to himself. Sam tried to engage him in a conversation about his unconventional relationship with Roni, but he kept her at arm's length. Not only was it none of her business, but he also really didn't want to dissect his feelings…especially not with his sister.

Halloween was a blast. Mark helped Roni turn the bakery into a haunted house by decorating upside-down cardboard boxes that had arrived with bulk baking supplies, and lassoing volunteers to hand out different kinds of cookies to the kids who stopped by. They turned the lights down low, and had spooky music on. Snoopy was the official mascot, guarding the door as a pirate. Parrot on his shoulder and all.

Roni had insisted that the event not be too scary, because the little ones deserved to have fun, too. Emma and Jack felt really special when Roni asked them to help hand out the treats. She was good at that, Mark realized. Making people feel good.

In November, Mark made a date with Roni to celebrate the second-month anniversary of her bakery opening. It was a little late, because they were both so busy, but he felt the moment deserved acknowledgment. He was so proud of all the work she'd done, the improvements she'd made to the store and, of course, the impact she'd had on this town. Two months in business, and she was already a staple in Butterscotch Ridge. Her name was on everyone's lips.

Of course, it wasn't *all* hunky-dory in Mark's world. The bakery was so busy, and Roni had to get up at an ungodly hour, which meant she turned in at an ungodly hour, as well. Mark didn't get nearly as much time with her as he'd like. And then, there were the jokes his friends made when they came into the bakery—at least, he assumed they were jokes—about how they all wanted to marry her and whisk her away to a secluded kitchen somewhere.

Roni laughed them off, when such comments were made in her presence, but Mark would grit his teeth to stop himself from responding. It wasn't because he felt insecure in his relationship with her… whatever it was.

All right. Maybe he did feel a little insecure. Maybe it bugged him that they weren't a *real* couple, that other men might see her as *available*. Maybe he did spend far too much time at night staring up at the ceiling and wishing he could have more with her. That he could talk her into redefining their relationship.

The trouble was, he wanted and needed her in his life. Couldn't see it without her. So in the end, after each bout of soul-searching, he knew he just had to suck it up. Be her friend with benefits—even though he was hungry for more—because she'd been clear about what she wanted and he'd agreed to her terms. With her history, he knew he'd done the right thing. He knew this was what she needed.

What he didn't admit, and never would, was how much it was starting to hurt.

In truth, they had everything a regular relationship had…except the commitment. He was greedy to want it all, and he knew it. But he did.

Sometimes, he entertained the idea of sitting her down and asking her for more, but he didn't, because if he did, she might end it all. If that made him a coward, so be it. Losing her was not an option. She was entwined in his life. She was *necessary.*

The night of their big date, she answered his knock with a huge smile and a kiss, and his heart swelled in a way that made his chest ache. "You look beautiful," he said, without even thinking. In fact, she had a glow about her.

"Thanks." She grinned and did a couple of poses, as though for a camera.

A skitter of long toenails sounded on the linoleum, and Snoopy zoomed into the room, so fast he couldn't make the turn and spun out into the fridge, all the while, barking his fool head off.

"Hey, Snoops," Mark said, leaning down to let him smell his hand before scratching the mutt on the head. "How's he doing?" he asked.

Roni snorted a laugh. "He's not *my* dog anymore." And, when Mark glanced up curiously, she added, "Gram. The two of them are inseparable. Probably because I'm too busy to scratch him all day, and she's happy to do it."

"That's good." He gave the pupper one more pat and stood. "Are you ready to go?"

"Yes." She grabbed a sweater, and hollered down the hall, "We're going, Gwen!"

"Okay," Gwen hollered back, over the sounds of some quiz show.

"It's nice of her to stay with Gram so you can get out. You deserve it," he said as they made their way down the stairs.

"Thanks. It's been crazy at the bakery. I'm so glad I have help now."

Mark bit back a smile. "Me, too. You work too hard."

"It's not work if you love it." She smiled at him again, and he felt it. That glow, shining and warm in his soul.

"I'm glad you're happy."

She didn't respond, other than to sigh and tuck her arm in his, but he could read her mood, so no words were necessary.

Dinner was perfect, even for the B&G. It would have been a romantic date, if he and Roni had been officially dating. They weren't. But at least everyone in the restaurant knew better than to stop by their table to chat. Well, almost everyone.

Chase came by to try to talk her into making pastries for his Sunday brunch, but Roni fed him a line about expanding on a schedule and shooed him away.

After Chase left them alone, he and Roni laughed and talked over their meals—a thick juicy steak for him, and an apple-walnut-and-gorgonzola salad for her. The champagne he'd ordered especially for the evening was a hit.

Roni smiled at him across the table. "You are so thoughtful. Thank you, Mark."

He lifted his flute to clink with hers. "This is a big deal."

Her gaze turned playful. "Is dinner and champagne all you have planned?" she asked. "Or do you have something else in mind?"

He knew exactly what she was hinting at. Heat

pooled in his groin. It had been far too long since they'd been together and alone. Still, he decided to play dumb. Just for fun. "Dessert?" he suggested.

Her lips curved into a smile. "My choice?"

He gave a little laugh. "I hear they have an excellent lemon cake tonight. Comes from that new bakery in town. You heard of it?"

She wrinkled her nose. "I'm not eating my own cake for dessert. Come on. Finish your steak. Let's go back to my place and I'll show you how I can really cook."

He had to comply. But he didn't finish his steak.

The walk back to her apartment took far too long and, in Mark's opinion, Gwen had way too much to say when they got back to Roni's place. He tried to be all casual and pretend he wasn't in a hurry for her to leave, but he was. He really was. The smell of Roni's perfume, the softness of her hair and the glint in her eye all promised to fill his rising need.

He wasn't expecting Roni's reaction when the door finally closed on Gwen's retreating form. She grabbed his hand and tugged him toward her room. "Come on," she said when he hesitated.

"Um… What about your grandmother?"

"What about her?" she said on a laugh.

"She's in the next room." He hadn't thought about that, but now he couldn't get it out of his head.

She shrugged. "We'll just be quiet. Like we've been doing, silly."

He nearly groaned. “I don’t think I can be quiet. Not tonight. Not when I’ve been thinking about this all day.”

For some reason, this made Roni smile. She wrapped her arms around his neck, leaned into him and went up on her toes to kiss him. And, man, what a kiss. All thoughts of grandmothers and being quiet fled from his mind.

It wasn’t until later, after, when she was asleep and he was awake, staring at the ceiling, that misgivings hit him once again.

Maybe Sam had been right. Maybe he was bound for heartbreak. But for now, he had Roni in his arms, and all was right with the world.

Chapter Nine

Roni woke up later than usual the next morning, and even though the sun was still asleep, Mark was gone. Her mood dipped, but then she heard his voice coming from the kitchen, along with the seductive scents of coffee and bacon.

She wrapped herself in her robe and padded into the kitchen. The scene there was heartwarming. Mark had made Gram a breakfast of bacon and scrambled eggs. How sweet.

"I had the strangest dream last night," Gram said to him as he brought her a cup of coffee.

"What was that?" he asked, even as his gaze flicked to Roni. His smile unfurled. It was a lover's smile. Sexy and delicious, a promise, perhaps. A delicious ribbon of excitement wove through her and she briefly wondered if they might have some time alone before she had to go down to the bakery.

Gram grabbed Mark's arm and pulled him closer, stealing his attention back. "I dreamed there were wolves," she said. "A pack of them, I think, howling. All night long."

It was adorable, the way his cheeks turned pink. The feral howls Gram had heard had, most likely, come from Roni's room.

Gram stood and shuffled in her slippered feet to the counter, where a tray of cookies awaited boxing. "Oh. What kind of cookies are these?" she asked.

"Shortbreads, Gram," Roni said.

Her face fell.

Roni opened the cookie jar, and fished out one of Gram's favorites. She always kept them on hand now. "But I have a molasses one right here if you'd like."

She gently pushed past Mark to grab the cookie, then left the room, happily nibbling her treat.

Mark chuckled. "She sure loves molasses cookies. But do you think she eats too many? She's got one every time I see her."

Roni had to smile. "The doctors say at her age, it's okay to splurge a little. And they make her so happy."

He grinned. "I wish a cookie could make me that happy."

"Me, too." Wouldn't it be wonderful if life was that easy?

"You hungry?" Mark asked, brandishing an empty plate.

"Starving." She shot him a grin. "Probably because of that workout last night."

He paused in scooping scrambled eggs onto her plate to waggle his brows. "That was fantastic."

"Even the howling?"

"I'm pretty sure you were the one doing the howling," he said as he set her breakfast before her and headed back to pour her a cup of coffee. Then he went and added a dollop of milk so it wouldn't be too hot. Good Lord, he was thoughtful. And kind. And patient. Probably the most perfect man on the planet.

He sat down next to her; his body was warm, comforting.

She inhaled deeply before she took a sip from her mug. The scents of coffee and hot man mingled. "Mmm. I could get used to this," she said.

He was close enough that she felt him go still. He caught her eye. "Really?"

His tone, the way he went on point, the intensity of his gaze…made little prickles dance over her nape. She decided to calm the sudden unease in her belly with a lighthearted joke.

"Having a man make me breakfast?" She took a bite of bacon. "Who wouldn't love that?" When he didn't respond, when his intensity didn't ease, she babbled on. "Besides, it's nice not being alone in the morning. Although, you could have woken me. We could have had a replay of last night." She sent him what she thought was a seductive expression, but he didn't react. Not the way she'd hoped, at any rate.

"Your grandmother was already awake," he said quietly.

She didn't understand his somber expression; it sent a sizzle down her solar plexus. It made her want to run. "Thank you for spending time with her," she said for want of something to say.

To her surprise, he took her hand in his. Stroked her with his thumb. Her apprehension grew.

But Mark didn't speak. Rather, he stared down at their entwined hands as though searching for words. All the while, her heart thudded as tension coiled within her like a spring.

Finally—*finally*—he met her gaze. Then he cleared his throat. "I love this thing we have," he said.

Ah, God. The sizzle returned. "I...love it, too," she said, because it was true and she didn't know what else to say. She suspected she knew what was coming and she dreaded it.

"Roni—"

"Mark. Don't." She had to stop him. She had to stop him before he asked her for something she couldn't give. Before he demanded the truth. "What we have is perfect." She even leaned in and kissed him, to make her point.

It broke her heart when he sighed. "Is it?"

It was perfect for her. She was blissfully happy for the first time in her life. She didn't want this to end. She didn't want this to change.

She knew it wasn't perfect for him. She'd known for a while. But she wasn't ready to have *this* conversation. Not today. So she pulled her hand from his, smiled and said, "It's getting late. I have to get to work, and so do you."

His stark expression shifted into a wash of emotion. There was anger in there. She could see it. Instinctively, she edged away. "To hell with work, Roni," he growled. "Nothing is as important to me as you are. Do you understand that? I love you. I want to be *with* you."

Roni's heart jumped. "You *are* with me." She cupped her hands around his face, thumbed away the dampness on his cheeks and tried to pretend they didn't burn like acid on her soul. "We're together nearly every night."

He shook his head. "I want more. Don't you want more, Roni?" And, when she didn't answer, he asked, "Don't you understand? I want more with you, Roni. A family, *children*."

Acid rose in her throat. She glanced at her wrist, saw the tremble. "It's getting late. I have a ton of stuff to do." She pushed away from the table, pulled her hand from his hold and stood. "Let's talk about this later."

"Roni—"

"Later," she said firmly, and then, before he could respond, she headed down the stairs to the bakery, leaving him all alone in an empty room.

* * *

"Well, did she say it was over?" Luke asked over his coffee.

Mark had gone straight to the B&G after he left Roni's—certainly not for an early-morning beer—and found his brother there having a late breakfast. The two of them sat at a semiprivate table at the back of the bar. Because it was between breakfast and lunch, they had most of the place to themselves, which was a good thing, given the topic. No one else needed to hear any of this. Mark had come to Luke after that disturbing conversation with Roni, because he hadn't known where else to go, and Luke and Roni seemed to have bonded over PTSD and pastries. Luke understood her in a way Mark could not. So, naturally, after his conversation with Roni, he'd turned to Luke.

But Luke's question was annoying, on so many levels. Mark frowned at him. "Were you even listening?"

Luke shrugged. "You knew what you were getting into. She was honest from the beginning."

Damn it, he hated when Luke was right.

"Just admit it." Luke shifted in his seat so he could lean closer. "You thought she was going to realize how perfect life is with you and magically change her mind about relationships. Didn't you?"

"No." But he had, hadn't he? "Are you saying this is my fault?"

Luke barked a laugh. “Who says anyone is at fault? The two of you are either a good fit, or you’re not.”

“We’re a perfect fit,” Mark snarled.

“Except you want marriage and she wants… What is it she wants?”

“I don’t know. Freedom?”

“Yeah, I’d guess safety over freedom, but there you go.”

This comment made Mark’s hackles rise; Luke was good at raising hackles. “She’s totally safe with me.”

Luke snorted. “You know that and I know that, but *she* doesn’t. Not really. Not deep down in her soul. That’s what PTSD really is. Lingering fear. Tough to root out.”

“I’ve never even lost my temper with her.” That fight they’d just had was as angry as he’d ever been with her, and it had mostly been frustration.

“Doesn’t matter. I remember feeling helpless after my injury, and I’m here to tell you, it’s not that easy to shake. She was in a brutally abusive relationship. She’s been through hell. I can’t imagine being battered on a daily basis, being constantly on edge. What that does to your heart and soul and body? You can’t blame her for trying to protect herself, for wanting to make sure that kind of thing never happens again.”

"How do I prove something like that? How do you prove a negative?"

"You shouldn't even try." Luke shrugged. "You should just be yourself."

"Which, clearly, isn't enough for her." He hated that his tone was so morose, but it was. It was his greatest fear come to life, not being enough.

Luke snorted. "You can't think that way. It's clear she loves you."

Did she? He knew she cared. She'd said as much. But caring was a far cry from love. "But maybe not enough to marry me."

"You need to accept the fact that she may never be ready for that. Ever."

Accept it? How did a man do that when he felt like this? It was hard loving her when she didn't feel the same. It hurt. "So you're saying I should just give up on marriage altogether?"

His brother gave a one-shouldered shrug. "Depends."

"On what?"

Luke's grin was crooked, his voice soft. "On whether you want to be with her or not."

And, yeah, that was the crux of the matter, wasn't it?

"You need to have a frank conversation, where you discuss what you each want from this relationship, and find some middle ground you can both be happy with."

Yeah. He understood what Luke was saying—a part of his soul already knew it. He had to make a decision. Did he love Roni enough to give her the space she needed and maybe even give up some of his own dreams for the woman he cared about so deeply?

It was time for him to make a decision that he would have to live with for the rest of his life.

After he left, Roni couldn't help stressing over that aborted fight with Mark. While she regretted running away from the conversation they needed to have, she had to acknowledge that she had good reasons. For one thing, she was confused about her feelings for Mark. He was the kind of man she'd always dreamed of finding. Handsome, smart, funny…gentle.

But her defense mechanisms had burrowed deep. She knew it was fear holding her back, and that irritated her. She wasn't a coward—she never had been. But, somehow, for some reason, she couldn't lean in to the concept of being in a real relationship. One with…commitment.

And now—so soon—Mark was talking marriage.

To be honest, it had freaked her out. She'd panicked. She'd overreacted. He'd been nothing but respectful. He'd let her take the lead each time, even though she could tell it cost him to hold back. And he'd been so flipping patient with her. He had done everything right.

Maybe it was only natural that he would start asking for more. Maybe she should never have even opened this door. The last thing she ever wanted to do was hurt him.

She loved everything about their relationship, especially the fact that there were no strings attached. She was free to walk away whenever she wanted to…

But did she? Want to walk away from him?

Never.

So where did this fear come from? Why did she resist making a commitment for something she wanted more than breath?

When she dug deep, and was really honest with herself, she knew.

She hadn't been honest with him. She hadn't told him the whole truth about the things Anthony had done to her. She hadn't shared the details of that horrible night when she'd lost her baby.

He obviously wanted children. She couldn't have them. And she was pretty sure, once Mark knew the truth, he wouldn't want to be with her anymore.

That was what she'd been protecting herself from.

But in protecting herself, she'd hurt him, the man she loved. And, yes, she loved him. There was no denying it.

If she told him the hard truth, she could lose it all,

and just thinking about it hurt more than she could bear. But she owed him the truth. He deserved to know everything, no matter how agonizing it would be for her to talk about it.

With her decision made, a weight lifted from her soul and she felt better. Oh, she still dreaded telling him and seeing his reaction. She clung to the possibility that he might not mind, as flimsy a prospect as it was. He wanted lots of children. She couldn't even give him one.

As always, she forced these dark thoughts from her mind, and focused on her work. She needed to get started on Thanksgiving pies, because the orders for those just kept coming in, but first she had to finish a project she'd been delighted to take on—a birthday cake for one of the Story Hour regulars who was turning six, one of Emma's little friends.

It had been so fun to plan out the superhero cake and decorate it with proportionately sized gum-paste characters—the stars of his favorite comic book. Roni smiled to herself as she piped speech bubbles with "pow," "wham" and "thwack" onto the sides of the cake in bright primary colors. She couldn't wait for Justin to see it at the party tonight.

In fact, she was generally excited about the party. Would Mark be there? He was friends with Justin's dad. Of course, a child's birthday party was not the venue for the conversation she needed to have with him, but maybe she could feel him out. Get a sense of how angry he'd really been when she'd shut him down. Like a coward.

She sighed heavily. She hadn't been fair with him, had she? Not from the beginning. He deserved better than—

Oh, dear. She realized it probably wasn't a good idea to think of Mark while she was supposed to be concentrating on her work. She pulled out a little palette knife to wipe away a frosting error and spent several minutes fixing it. She was so focused, she didn't even look up when the bell over the door rang.

"Well, well, well. Look at you."

Roni froze. Her heart clenched at the sound of that deep, familiar voice. Her hand clenched around the piping bag, too, and icing spurted out, all over her carefully created masterpiece. From his spot curled up on the divan on the other side of the shop, Snoopy growled low in his throat.

She stared at the mess she'd made for a blind moment. Then fury rose and overcame her fear. She whirled and glowered at her ex-husband. "What the hell are you doing here?"

Anthony stepped back, eyes wide. It occurred to her that she'd never snarled at him before—he'd preferred it when she was submissive and silent.

She wasn't submissive anymore. "Well?"

It took a second for him to collect himself, to morph back into the man she remembered—big, superior, intimidating. It was an odd thing to see, watching him *become* a predator right before her eyes. But she saw something else. She saw that moment, that flicker in his eye, where he'd felt doubt.

And that was all she needed.

When he leaned forward, crowding her in the way he always did, she stood her ground.

"You had to know I would come for you as soon as they let me out." His breath was warm, moist against her cheek. Still, she stared him down.

"Why *did* they let you out?" Surely it was way too early.

A smile uncoiled on his face; in that moment, he looked like the cat that had caught the canary. And she was the canary. "Good behavior," he said in a smug tone.

"Well, you need to leave."

He grabbed her arm and whipped her around—her back to his chest, his arms locked around her as he whispered in her ear. "But I missed you, *honey*." His tone was cold as steel, and for a moment, she felt as helpless as ever in his grip.

But she remembered how much time she'd spent fighting her way back, healing her wounds in body and mind. Coming back here. Building a life of her own. She'd vowed to never be under anyone's thumb again, to never be helpless again.

She'd be damned if she'd let him take everything away from her.

As though he heard her thoughts, his hold tightened and he said, "You're mine, Veronica. You always will be."

After their heart-to-heart, Luke gave Mark some space, wandering over to check in with Chase and the barflies while Mark nursed his coffee and thought things through. He knew, beyond a shadow of a doubt, that he loved Roni. What he was struggling with was releasing the expectations he'd carried all his life—that love would lead to marriage. That marriage meant two people belonged to each other, whatever that meant. That they promised each other forever, or at least a reasonable facsimile.

Roni didn't want to belong to anyone for a minute, much less forever. He wondered, honestly, how easy it might be for him to adjust his thinking on something he'd been raised to believe—if it could mean sharing some kind of life with the woman he loved.

He knew it wouldn't be an easy process, working through this, hence this seat in the back of the bar. One would have thought that people would leave him alone so he could work through his conflicting feelings. It only made sense. If *he* saw someone hunched over a table in the back of a bar, *he'd* leave them alone.

Sophia Cage had another idea. She walked through the door, and the second she spotted him, she homed in on him like a ballistic missile, sashaying over to his table with a seductive smile on her face. "Hey, handsome." She sat down without asking and her expensive perfume washed over him.

Roni smelled like oranges, lemons sometimes. Roni smelled bright and fresh and sweet.

But it was pointless to compare the two. Roni would always win.

"What are you doing back here?" Sophia asked, setting her hand on his knee.

He caught her wrist, removed her hand. "I need to think, so I came here to be alone." He was hoping she'd take the hint and leave.

She tipped her head to the side, wriggled free from his grip and set her palm on his chest instead. "It looks to me like you need some company. And here I am."

He sighed. "Soph, I need to be alone. Okay?"

She edged back, caught his gaze. "You liked my company before."

He'd liked a lot of women's company before. Too many, maybe. But now? Now there was only one.

As he stared at Sophia, conviction solidified in his mind and heart and soul. Yeah. He wasn't going to let Roni go, and he knew it. He couldn't.

Whatever she wanted, he would give her. And as for his insecurities about not having that ring on her finger, he would just have to trust her. The same way she trusted him to not act like her ex. Because that's what real love was. Trust. Faith in one another.

He'd give that to her. And, somehow, he knew she'd give him the same in return. And it didn't matter what they called it.

His heart lifted, and he smiled at Sophia. "Thanks," he said as he stood and dropped a ten on the table for the coffees.

She gaped at him. "Thanks? What for?"

But he didn't answer. He nodded to Luke and made a beeline out the door, heading to Roni's place down the block.

Luke caught up with him at the corner, because Mark had to wait for a truck at the intersection. "What are you gonna do?" he asked.

"What do you think?" He shot his brother a wry grin. "I'm gonna fold."

To which Luke barked a laugh. "It's not the folding, bro. It's knowing when to."

"Right." Mark nodded and crossed the street, but the paused when he heard a ruckus coming from the bakery.

"Is that Snoopy?" Luke asked.

It was. And the dog was barking up a storm. The brothers shared a glance and then set off for the store, Luke's injured leg keeping him a few paces behind Mark.

As Mark came up on the big windows of the bakery, he saw Roni in the grip of another man. His arms were around her shoulders, and while Mark couldn't hear the words, he could definitely tell that he was shouting at her. Horror skittered through his gut. Instinctively, he knew who the man was, but he didn't stop to take it in, not now.

"Call Cole," he barked at Luke as he sprinted for the door.

He was still too late to save her.

Because, it appeared, she'd already saved herself.

It took his brain a second to process the scene, but when it did, he realized that Roni had just thrown a full-grown man over her shoulder and onto the hard floor of the bakery. He was now lying on the ground, groaning. She stood over him, arms akimbo, breathing heavily. Snoopy, for his part, took a position between Roni and the threat, and continued to issue threatening growls.

Roni glanced up and their gazes clashed. He was ready to run to her, to comfort her...but there was no need. She simply glowed.

"It worked," she said, with her eyes alight. "I learned it in a self-defense class, but I've never done it for real. I can't believe it worked."

"Good for you," Luke said.

Mark gaped at them both, speechless. Why were they high-fiving? Why were they not focused on the man sprawled on the floor? Why was he here? What the hell had she even been doing, fighting him for Christ's sake? A man like that could have snapped her neck like a twig. Fear for her roiled with rising acid and ire in his gut.

"What the hell do you think you're doing?" he shouted.

Roni froze. She seemed taken aback for a second, but only for a second. Then she stood right up to him and responded with equal ferocity. "Protecting myself."

Heat and horror rose within him. "You could have been hurt!"

"But she wasn't."

It was all Mark could do not to deck his brother. "And who the hell is this?" he asked, nodding at the crumpled fellow on the floor.

Before Roni could answer, the bastard levered himself into a sitting position and glared at her with a malevolence Mark had never seen in anyone's expression before.

"He's my *ex*-husband," she said with the emphasis on the *ex*. And, yeah. His suspicions were confirmed. This was Anthony. The man who had traumatized her, beaten her. Thrown her through a plate glass shower door. Cut her to ribbons. Nearly killed her. "And he needs to leave. Now." Her voice was clear and strong.

"The hell?" Anthony snapped, struggling to his feet. "I'm not leaving. You are still my wife, *Veronica*." The way he said her name sent shivers down Mark's spine.

"It's Roni. And we're divorced. We've been divorced for two years."

He leaned in and growled, "You *belong to me*."

Mark saw the shudder run through her. Still, she stood up to Anthony. Didn't matter that this creep probably had a hundred pounds on her. Her courage scared Mark to death, knowing what this man was capable of.

Anthony took a step toward Roni, and Mark put himself between them, but before he could land that first satisfying punch in Anthony's too-smug face, Snoopy lunged forward and grabbed the cretin's cuff, snarling and growling all the while. Anthony looked down. "What the hell is that?" he said as he took a swipe at the pup with a shiny loafer. Snoopy skidded across the floor with a pained yelp.

Roni went utterly still. Her eyes narrowed on Anthony, her expression eerily calm, cold. She stepped around Mark to face her ex again. He tried to hold her back, but she gently set her hand on his arm and extricated herself from his hold. "No," she said with a frigid intensity that made Anthony retreat. It made little hairs prickle on Mark's nape, as well. "You do not kick my dog. You do not kick me. You do not kick anyone. Do you hear me?"

Something about her demeanor hit home with Anthony, too. His eyes widened. He backed away.

She followed.

And then, Snoopy joined in, dancing around his feet and going in for an ankle bite here and there.

"Stop. Stop!" Anthony howled. He shot an imploring glance at Mark. "Help me, damn it."

The only reason Mark stepped in was because he was afraid that Anthony might take a swipe at Roni, or another one at Snoopy. He took Roni in his arms, and whispered, "It's okay. It's okay. I'm here."

She glanced at him with blank eyes—a sliver of icy fear sliced through him at that sight—but then her gaze cleared and she saw him. "He kicked my dog, Mark," she said. "Did you see? He kicked my dog."

"I saw, honey, I saw. Don't worry. I'm here."

"And who the hell are you?"

Mark's gaze whipped back to Anthony, who was jabbing a finger at him with each word. Though, Mark noticed, he was careful; he didn't come too close. *Coward.*

Mark had no intention of answering that question—partly because he didn't know what word to use, didn't really know what he was to Roni—so he was surprised when she spoke up.

"He's the man I love," she said, loud and clear enough for the next county to hear.

His heart zigged upward and he grinned at her. "I am?"

Her smile softened. "You know you are, Mark." Then she went up on her toes and kissed him.

He kissed her back.

He was vaguely aware of Anthony sputtering at

them in the background, and Snoopy still yapping like he'd trapped a fox. But mostly he was aware of Roni. Her scent, her taste, the way she felt so perfect in his arms. "I love you," he told her.

"I love you, too."

But Anthony wasn't done. His hand fell heavily on Mark's shoulder. "Get away from her, you—"

Before Anthony could say another word, Mark whirled and clocked him.

Chapter Ten

Anthony hit the ground with a thud.

"I didn't see that," Cole said from the doorway.

"See what?" Luke said, even as he offered Mark a high five.

Cole snorted a laugh and shook his head before pulling out his pad. "Right. So what's going on here?"

Mark glanced at Roni. This was her story to tell, after all. She nodded and waved toward Anthony's form. "My ex just got out of jail for spousal assault and involuntary manslaughter. He came here to find me. When he grabbed me, I threw him over my shoulder."

Cole's eyes widened; he sized up Roni with a new appreciation.

But then, Mark realized what she'd just said. He hadn't ever asked her for the details of her ordeal, so he had no idea what she'd meant. He turned her into his arms and stared into her eyes. "Manslaughter?" A whisper.

She nodded. Tears filled her eyes. "I was pregnant the last time he assaulted me. The baby died."

She said it so matter-of-factly, but he saw—no, *felt*—the pain that wracked her. "Oh, Roni..." It was all he could manage. That and a hug he didn't want to ever end.

"Well, okay." Cole's jaw flexed as he focused on Anthony, who'd levered into a sitting position on the floor, showing the good sense not to get up again. "Did you just get out of prison?" he asked in a cool, detached, professional kind of voice.

Anthony scowled. "A couple weeks. Look, I just came to talk to my wife—"

"I'm no longer your wife."

"Veronica." Again, Anthony's tone made the little hairs on Mark's nape prickle. It was a toxic slurry of domination and condescension. His fingers flexed for no reason whatsoever. Certainly not with the desire to fist together and clobber someone again. "Veronica, come here." Anthony pointed to a spot right in front of him, as though he were ordering a dog.

Her throat worked, but other than that, and a scorching glare, she didn't respond.

Good for her.

"You on probation?"

Anthony's expression turned even more sour at Cole's query. "She's my *wife*."

Cole ignored this insistence and turned his attention on Roni. "Did you file for a restraining order?"

She nodded. "I filed one in Seattle and another with the county when I moved over here."

"Okay." Cole's smile widened. "That's all I need to take him in."

Roni gaped at him. "Really?"

"Yeah. Violating a restraining order is a violation of parole." He shrugged. "No problem."

"Wait. I just want to talk to my wife— Hey!" Anthony struggled against being handcuffed and snarled and scowled, but frankly, watching Cole cuff him and lead him down the street to the substation made Mark's day. The only downside was the fact that as soon as Anthony disappeared from sight, Roni started shaking.

Mark knew she was in shock. Because no matter what, facing down her ex had to have been gutting. He glanced at Luke, who read his mind. While Luke locked up the bakery, Mark took Roni upstairs and gave her a glass of sherry, because that was the only alcohol he could find in the apartment, and even that was probably twenty years old, judging from the crystalized sugar on the lid. He sat her on the sofa in the living room, pulled her close and held her as she sipped. Snoopy, of course, positioned himself on her lap. It was natural, Mark supposed, for her fingers to stroke the pup's warm belly.

When Luke came upstairs, he poked his head into the room. "Milly's still napping. You got this?" He nodded at Roni.

Mark held her closer. "Yeah. We're good."

"Okay then. I'm gonna take off." And, to Roni, he said, "You did great, honey. You did real good."

She murmured, "Thanks," and he sketched a wave and left.

Silence filled the room. Mark passed the moments rubbing Roni's back as she worked through her emotions. He could practically *feel* her pass from one to the next. Fear, anger, exhilaration.

It scared him, because she'd been lucky this time. Her reaction had taken Anthony by surprise. Who knew what he would have done if Mark and Luke hadn't shown up when they did? After she'd freaking thrown him to the ground?

He could easily have picked himself up and come at her again…this time, enraged. He could easily have hurt her. Maybe killed her. It wasn't as if they doubted he was capable. She—

His thoughts stalled as he realized she'd pulled back and was staring at him.

"What?" he asked.

"Are you okay?" she asked in a soft voice.

"Am *I* okay?" He laughed through a frustrated snort. "Are *you* okay?"

"You're the one who's all tense and muttering things beneath his breath."

"I'm not muttering."

"You are." Her smile took much of the sting out of the accusation.

He sighed heavily. “Yeah, you’re right. I’m not okay.”

She tipped her head to the side. “All right. Just say it.”

“You scared me to death, Roni, going at him like that. He could have lashed out at you. You could have been hurt.”

“But I wasn’t.”

He glowered. “Don’t start that again.”

“He kicked my dog, Mark. What does that mean to you?”

“That he’s a bastard. That he’ll go after anything that’s weaker than he is. That doesn’t mean he’s not dangerous. Please, please, don’t ever do that again. Don’t even confront him like that. *He could have hurt you.*” He had to stress that last bit, because he wanted to make sure he got his emotions across.

She sighed heavily. “He has hurt me. So many ways, so many times. I have had enough.”

He wrapped her in his arms and rested his head against hers. “I’m so sorry about the baby, Roni. I wish I knew what to say to make it better.”

She rubbed his arm. “I’m sorry, too. I will always hold that baby in my heart. I will. But we can’t let death keep us from living, can we? If anything, I need to live better, to make her proud.”

“It was a girl?” His eyes teared up. “A little girl?” She snuggled closer.

“Are you mad at me?” she asked.

He gaped at her. "How could I be mad at you? Seeing you face him down… I've never been more scared."

She met his gaze. He hated that hers was wet, that her eyes glinted with some emotion he couldn't quite identify. "You've always been there for me."

"I'm not your ex, Roni." The bastard didn't even deserve a name.

"No." She put her hand to his cheek and stared at him openly. "No, you're not. You're nothing like him. You are gentle and sweet and you've been more patient than I ever imagined a man could be."

He tightened his hold on her. "You told him I was the man you loved," he reminded her, just in case she'd forgotten.

Her eyes glinted. "I meant it. You are the man I love, Mark Stirling. For better or for worse."

His heart hiccuped. "Hey, back up, woman. Them's marrying words." He meant it as a joke, but she wasn't playing around at all. Her expression went all solemn and sober.

"I know."

Heat rose in his belly; the words spun in his head. "What are you saying?" He barely got the words out.

Again, that playful smile. "If you still want more, I'm here. But there's something you should know before you—"

"There's nothing I need to know. Marry me."

She shook her head and pulled away. "Hear me out. Then, if you want, ask again. This is important."

When he nodded, she removed Snoopy from her lap, took Mark's hand, pulled him off the couch and led him into the kitchen.

"This conversation is going to require some fortification," she told him with a brave smile; it only wobbled a little.

He tried to smile back, but his heart wasn't in it. He could tell from her expression, whatever this was, it ran deep. A wound that cut deep into her soul.

All he knew was, it didn't matter what it was. He would love her regardless.

Roni dawdled around in the kitchen for longer than it took to make a pot of coffee and cut some brownies, but she needed the time to build up her resolve. The last thing she wanted was to share this secret with anyone, much less Mark Stirling. But he deserved to know the truth. Especially if he wanted to marry her.

Hopefully, he wouldn't take it too hard.

Finally, she turned to the table, where he was waiting. Patiently. She set his coffee and plate in front of him and then went back for her own. But after that, there was no more avoiding anything. She sat with a sigh.

He reached across the table and took her hand,

and she let him, because she needed it. "I can tell this is difficult for you," he said.

She nodded. "It is."

He shrugged and took a sip of his coffee. "Take your time. I have a brownie."

He was joking, of course, but she appreciated it.

"When Anthony went after me, when he went after Snoopy, it brought back…a memory." Even now, it engulfed her, took her back. Put her in that bathroom amid shattered glass and a rain of agony pelting down on her—

Mark's thumb stroked her skin, bringing her back, blissfully, to this room. "He kicked me, too, you see," she said without meeting his gaze.

"He kicked you?" His fingers tightened on hers. A muscle in his cheek flexed.

"More than once. He did. Here." She cradled a hand over her belly. "I didn't fight back. I couldn't. All I could think about was protecting the baby."

"God. I'm so sorry."

"Me, too. But that's not all. That night, in the ER, when they told me about the baby…"

He held her closer. "I'm here."

"They said my…uterus was damaged."

Silence settled. He stroked her with his thumb.

"I can't… There are no…" She sighed. "Mark, I can't have another baby."

He stared up at her, tears welling in his eyes. "Sweetheart…"

She brushed back his hair, looped it behind his ear. "I know you want kids. I'm sorry. I understand if that changes things. I do." *But, please, God, don't let it change things.*

Oh, it was an eternity, that moment, with him staring at her working through her confession, changing his life and hers in that second or two. And then he stood and pulled her up with him, took her in his arms and held her, and she let him.

"Hey," he said into her hair. "There are so many other options for kids. So many in foster care. So many kids who need a good home."

She pulled back and stared at him. Her heart thundered. "You'd be okay with that?"

His grin warmed her. Oh, how it warmed her. "Hun, I am open to anything…if it makes you happy."

"You deserve to have your own kids, though. With your genes…"

"Then surrogacy. We'll look into it. We'll look into whatever it takes."

"But, Mark—"

He didn't let her continue. Didn't let her argue with him, even though she wasn't sure why she tried. He kissed her and kissed her hard. "It doesn't matter, Roni. Not to me. The only thing that matters to me is that we found our way back to each other. I don't want to lose you ever again. So it's you and me. That's what matters. That's all."

She smiled as she met his gaze. “Why do you always have to be so perfect, Mark Stirling?” she asked.

His face split into an enormous grin and he shrugged. “In the blood, I guess.” He leaned back. “Wait—so does that mean you’ll marry me?”

Her smile grew wider. “Yes, Mark. I’ll marry you.” And then she laughed at the pure joy in his expression. She had to.

Mark and Roni stayed up talking long into the night. He instinctively knew she needed to work through her feelings, and so did he.

But damn, it was hard to listen as she told him all the dirty details of her marriage. Anthony was just down the street in the cell at the substation. It wouldn’t take long to march down there and punch him again. Maybe more than once.

It was a good thing Roni needed him here, and he needed her. The feel of her warm body curled in his arms, the sight of her adoring gaze… She renewed him, each and every day.

He knew, beyond a shadow of a doubt, that he’d made the right decision to ask for her hand, and she’d made the right decision to accept. They were going to be happy together, because both of them understood it was their responsibility—both of them—to make it so.

Funny, wasn’t it? He’d been a lone wolf for so

long, only responsible for his own happiness. What a hollow little world he'd carved out for himself.

And he'd defended it!

What a moron.

This was so much better. This…partnership.

He was also excited about the possibility that someday they would have a child or two—either through surrogacy or adoption. And while either process probably wouldn't be easy, it was possible.

Anything was possible now.

He watched dawn break, holding Roni close and smiling at her adorable snores. He wanted to wake her, he wanted to make love to her, but yesterday had been a long day. He decided to let her sleep in. Maybe make her breakfast in bed.

The kitchen was shadowed as he padded, barefoot, to the coffee maker. He wore the flannel lounge pants he'd brought over to Roni's when the nights started getting chilly, but he hadn't pulled on his T-shirt before leaving the bedroom. It wasn't a strange thing for him to wander around his place half-dressed, so he didn't think twice about it…until someone knocked on the door.

Not to put too fine a point on it, until he opened the door…to Gwen.

He had to fight the urge to cover himself like a Gothic virgin caught in flagrante delicto. Tough to do when Gwen stared at his naked chest and her nose curled.

"Really?" she muttered.

He opened the door wider. "Come on in, Gwen. I was making coffee. You want some?"

"Not really. Is Roni available?"

"She's sleeping in."

"She owns a bakery. People who own a bakery don't get to sleep in."

"Carlos and Lupe are covering the mornings now."

Gwen frowned. Or maybe it was just her usual expression. "Oh, yeah. She mentioned she'd hired more staff."

"They're working out great. She actually has time on her hands now."

"Good."

She stood there awkwardly as they both watched the coffee dribble into the pot. "You sure you don't want some?" he asked as he poured a cup for himself.

"I suppose."

He pulled another mug from the cupboard, filled it and set it on the table for her. "I'm, ah, actually glad you're here, Gwen," he said as he sat. He pretended not to notice the face she pulled. "I'd like to talk to you about something."

"Great." She dropped into a chair, then fixed her coffee with cream and sugar.

"It's about Roni."

She sent him a surprised look, but it was probably just sarcasm. She was real good at sarcasm.

"I know you're not a fan of mine—"

"Cut to the chase, Stirling."

"But Roni cares for you a lot, and I know you care for her, too."

"She's the closest I've ever had to a sister. And she's had a raw deal her whole life."

"You're protective of her."

"Damn straight."

"And I appreciate that."

"I'm not doing it for *you*, you know." For someone who wanted him to cut to the chase, she sure wasn't making it easy.

Okay, fine.

"I've asked her to marry me, and she said yes."

Well, that shut her up. She froze, the mug halfway to her mouth—which was agape. And she stared at him for so long, he started feeling self-conscious about being half-naked again.

"You what?" she finally burbled.

"Roni and I are getting married. I want her to be happy. You make her happy. I was just hoping the two of us could work things out so she won't have to deal with any tension between us. To that end, I'd like to apologize for whatever I did to hurt you or make you mad."

Her eyes narrowed. "You have no idea, do you?"

Not a clue. "Sorry."

She drew in a deep breath and gusted a sigh. "Polly Baxter."

He stared at her, waiting for more. It didn't come. "Polly Baxter?"

Something in his tone must have irritated her. Her knuckles on the mug handle went white. "She was one of my best friends. Do you not even remember her?"

"Of course I do. She sat behind me in algebra class."

"She *tutored* you in algebra class." Why'd she make tutoring sound dirty?

He shrugged. "Okay. She *tutored* me. What is this about, Gwen?"

"Don't you remember?"

Apparently not. "Help me out here, would you?"

She rolled her eyes. "You dated her, you jackass."

"What...?" Oh. Oh, right. "I took her to dinner at the B&G. After I passed the final exam. A thank-you for her help. It wasn't a date."

"She thought it *was* a date. It broke her heart when you just dropped her."

"I didn't drop her. School ended, summer started, I was busy at the ranch. Like every summer."

"Not too busy to date Pam Kryzinski."

Wow. This wasn't going to end, was it?

"Gwen, I'm sorry Polly thought we were on a date. I'm sorry if I hurt her feelings. That was not my intention. Would it help if I apologized to her directly?"

Her eyes widened. "Good God, no. She'd be mortified."

What? Why? He'd never understand this conversation if he lived to be a hundred. "What can I do to make this better? What are you really worried about?" he asked bluntly.

She frowned. "That should be clear."

"Humor me."

"Fine. I'm worried that you'll get tired of Roni, just like you've always done with every other girl you dated in this town. I'm worried you'll leave her for someone else and break her heart."

Wow. He supposed, after dating as many years as he had, he should've expected someone to rake him over the coals at some point. But still. He didn't expect it to burn quite this badly.

He met Gwen's gaze and held it. "Gwen, I'm all in with Roni. I love her so much, it sometimes hurts. No one else comes even close. No one. I know there's nothing I can say to convince you that I've changed, but I have." He sighed heavily. "I wish there was something I could do to make things right between us."

As she mulled this over, she frowned at him, then took a sip of her coffee. At long last, she sighed and glanced at the countertop. "I suppose you could get me a cookie."

He bounded to his feet, rummaged through the cookie jar and brought her a Lemon Sandie. He knew better than to touch the molasses ones.

She accepted it with a hint of vindication, but just a hint. "Thank you," she said starchily.

"You're welcome." And then, halfway through the cookie, she added, "And you could also offer to babysit once in a while."

He swallowed heavily—a gulp really. Gwen's kids were a handful. "Ah, sure. Yes. Of course. Anytime."

"Saturday at six?"

His mind raced. But really, what could he say? "Sure."

But when she smiled at him, a real smile, he knew he'd said the right thing. He'd made peace with Gwen. And it felt good.

Thanksgiving Day dawned bright and crisp. Roni was excited because she, Mark and Gram were going to the ranch for a big family dinner. She'd never been excited about Thanksgiving before—she'd always hated turkey and cranberries, and neither her mother nor her father had made a big deal of it. It had been just like any other meal. The three of them sitting around the table in relative peace until a fight broke out. With Anthony, most meals had been clinical in nature, very little conversation over the quiet clatter of silverware.

It had to be the *family* part of the family dinner that made her so excited. With the Stirlings involved, it felt like…an event. And, as usual, she expressed her joy by baking. Even after making over a hundred pumpkin pies, *this one* was still fun. It was for people she loved.

She also made brownies for Luke, a lemon cake for Dorthea and an extra batch of molasses cookies for Gram. And, of course, a sweet-potato pie with candied bacon. That one almost didn't get made because Mark kept sneaking in and stealing the bacon. And if it wasn't Mark, it was Snoopy, the little thief.

The other reason she might have been giddy was because she and Mark had decided that it was time to share their engagement with the family. In addition to being excited, she was scared to death that they would be disappointed. She didn't dare put that fear into words, but it did hover like a black cloud.

It was easy to forget when she, Gram and Mark headed out for the morning's activities—the dinner at the ranch wasn't until evening. This morning they reported to the B&G, along with a lot of other volunteers, to help with Chase's favorite event—delivering turkey dinners to senior citizens and families in the area who needed or wanted help. Roni wasn't surprised to see Sam, Lizzie and Emma pulling in to pick up their deliveries as she and Mark pulled out. They shared a wave in passing and then Mark turned onto the eastbound road. "I love this idea," Roni said to the space between the two front seats—she'd taken the back because the front was easier for Gram to get in and out of.

Mark nodded. "I help every year. For one thing, it reminds you how lucky you are, and at the same time, reminds other people that someone does care."

"And it's a nice day for a drive," Gram added.

It was a good thing it was a nice day for a drive, because most of their stops were far-flung places. Gram insisted on getting out at each house and greeting the recipients personally. In some cases, that meant long chats and reminiscences. At one point, Mark had to call a halt to the catching up because it was getting late and they had to get back to the ranch for their own meal.

Roni was happy that she'd been able to provide something helpful to the outreach program. She was still glowing when Mark pulled into the Stirling Ranch driveway. She carried the goodies she'd made as Mark helped Gram up the stairs to the front porch. As always, her heart swelled as she marveled on how gentle and thoughtful he was.

And he loved her, just as she was. Something to be thankful for, indeed.

* * *

Sam met them at the door, and quickly took half of Roni's load. "Come on in. We're staging food in the kitchen. Milly, Grandma is waiting for you in the parlor."

"Oh, excellent." Milly reclaimed her arm and headed in that direction, so Mark turned and followed Sam and Roni into the kitchen.

"Wow," he said as the full aroma of the meal smacked him in the face. His salivary glands went into overdrive. "How much food is this?"

Roni glanced at him over her shoulder and laughed. "It is a ridiculous amount of food," she said.

He nodded, but it was a purely instinctive reaction. The rest of him—his heart, mind and soul—was focused on one thing. That look in her eye. It wasn't the kind of come-hither glance that might have attracted him in the past. It was a come-hither-and-love-me-forever-and-I-will-love-you-forever-too glance. He couldn't not turn her to face him, cup her cheeks in his hands and kiss her soundly.

He could have kissed her forever, but his sister passed by, muttering, "Get a room."

"Roni's here! Roni's here!" Emma bellowed as she spotted them. She stopped short and took in the sight of Roni in Mark's arms. "What are you doing?" she asked of no one and everyone.

"Kissing Roni," he said, with more than a hint of pride.

Emma wrinkled her nose. "Why?"

He released Roni and ruffled Emma's hair. "Because I can, kiddo."

Emma wrinkled her nose. "My mom and dad do that, too," she said. "It's really gross."

"I brought pumpkin pie," Roni said, perhaps to earn back her lost esteem in Emma's eyes for kissing. It worked.

"Oooh. Let me see!"

Roni opened the Tupperware container to show off a beautiful pie, which had an elaborately decorated turkey cutout—made of piecrust—on the top. It had pink and purple feathers, which were Emma's favorite colors. A much smaller turkey followed the first. "What do you think?"

Emma stared for a long while and then gazed up at Roni in awe. "Oh, I think it's the most perfectest thing I ever saw."

"Do you know what this is?" Roni pointed at the tiny turkey.

Emma shook her head.

Roni leaned closer and whispered, "It's your puppy, following right behind you. See? It's Daisy."

Emma's jaw dropped and then she started laughing. "Don't tell anyone," she said to Roni. "It'll be a surprise."

"What a great idea," Roni said in an equally conspiratorial tone. She glanced at Mark and grinned. No one else cared about the decoration on the pie, but it didn't matter, because she'd done it for Emma.

She watched as the sprite ran from the room bellowing, "Mom, guess what!"

Mark chuckled as he slipped his arm around her shoulders and held her close to his side. Where *he* belonged.

Then Luke burst into the room. Luke didn't usually burst into rooms, but whatever. "Hey! Roni!" he said, stealing her for a hug. The moment he could do so without making things awkward, Mark took her back. "Emma said you were here."

"Here I am. Mark, too." She patted him on the chest as though to remind his brother of his existence.

"Yeah. So Emma said you brought turkey pie?"

She chuckled. "Pumpkin pie."

"With a turkey decoration," Mark clarified.

Roni turned and headed toward the foyer, then said over her shoulder, "I made brownies for you."

Luke's "Yee-haw" rocked the rafters.

"Well," Mark said as he caught up with her, "you made somebody happy."

"It's what I live for," she replied, and then eased off her coat. She'd worn it all day while they'd been delivering meals, so he hadn't noticed what she was wearing underneath—a sleeveless dress. As he took the garment from her and hung it on the coat tree by the door, something clogged in his throat. Maybe in his eyes, too.

When he turned back to her, her hand rose and hovered, as though she had the urge to cover herself, her scars, but after a moment, she dropped it.

“You look so beautiful tonight,” he said, tracing a gentle line across her shoulder. When he caught her eye, her gaze was a little damp. How brave she was.

“Thank you,” she said. And he had to kiss her again.

“Oh, gawd,” Sam muttered as she passed by. “If the two of you can unclinch, it’s time to eat.”

Laughing, Mark and Roni made their way to the dining room table with the rest of the clan. Once everyone was seated and had beverages, DJ stood and raised his glass. “I think this is the time where we all share what we are especially thankful for.”

“You start,” Sam said.

“Okay.” DJ bowed his head for a moment and then said, “I am thankful that Danny, Lizzie and Emma have joined our family. It’s great to have you here with us, my brother.”

“Hear! Hear!” Mark said with a grin at Danny’s blush.

“Oh, oh, oh!” Emma cried. “Me next!” She lifted her juice. “I’m thankful for having a dad.”

"Aw, that's sweet, hon," Danny said. "I'm thankful for—"

"Wait!" Emma bellowed. "I have another thankful-for."

"Okay." Danny set down his wine.

"I'm also thankful for my uncle Luke for giving me his bone marrow."

This, of course, earned her a hug from Luke, who was seated at her side. "I'm thankful for you, too, munchkin."

"And I'm thankful for my aunt and uncles and Daisy and everyone," she announced, mid-hug.

Lizzy was thankful for Emma's health and the new baby, Dorthea was thankful for tea parties with her granddaughter and Gram was thankful for a bakery that always carried fresh molasses cookies.

"And how about you, Mark?" DJ asked when it came round the table to him.

His heart jumped. Heat crawled up his cheeks. His breath caught. "Well," he said, lifting his glass. "I am thankful—very thankful—that Roni has agreed to marry me."

He barely had the words out before everyone cheered. They all hopped up—except for Luke, who came over with measured steps because his leg was bothering him—and surrounded Mark and Roni with congratulations and hugs.

It meant a lot to him, but he knew, somehow he knew, it meant so much more to Roni.

"I love you," he said, and she responded in kind.

It might work out after all, this commitment thing. With love, they might do okay.

The cacophony around her was overwhelming, but for once, Roni didn't shrink away from it. This was good energy. Good chaos. It was a gift, and she knew it.

"So you're gonna get married?" Emma asked as she finished her second helping of sweet potatoes and candied bacon.

Roni couldn't stop her grin. "Yes." *Yes.* It excited her each time she thought of it.

Emma glanced pointedly at Roni's hand, and frowned. "Really? Where's the ring?"

"I don't have a ring yet," she said.

Emma snorted. "Then you're not engaged. Not really."

"We are." She felt their eyes on her, though her eyes were on Mark. His expression warmed her heart. "Rings don't mean anything. Nothing means anything, except love."

Danny pulled Lizzie into a side-hug and kissed her forehead. "Amen."

DJ and Luke nodded. Dorthea lifted her glass. Gram clasped her hand on her chest. "How sweet."

Sam, however, snorted. "No ring, though?"

"I'm getting her a ring," Mark muttered. "We *just* made the decision. We thought you'd want to know before it showed up in that online newsletter Gladys Henry does."

Luke lifted an eyebrow, along with his beer. "Did this decision have anything to do with your visitor at the bakery?" he asked Roni.

"What visitor?" Sam made a face. She hated being left out of the action. But Roni had been so busy preparing for Thanksgiving, they hadn't had a chance to talk.

"Anthony, my ex, came to the bakery last week," Roni said.

"And Roni took him *down*." Leave it to Luke to crow and spike a dinner roll like a football player after a touchdown.

"What do you mean, *she took him down*?" Emma asked.

Luke stilled. Flushed. "Um..."

"Yeah," Lizzie said, clocking her head to the side. "What exactly do you mean, Luke?"

He glanced from Lizzie to Emma and back again. His lips moved as he tried to escape from this hole.

Roni decided to save him. "Emma, he was not nice, so I had to give him a time-out."

"That's one way of putting it," Mark murmured.

"Cole's got him in the cooler for parole violation." Luke shrugged. "I assume they're gonna ship him right back to whatever hole he crawled out of."

Enough of this. Anthony was *not* invited to dinner.

"Who wants dessert?" Roni asked. And then she laughed because their enthusiasm was delightful. When Mark followed her to the kitchen to help with the dessert, he pulled her into his arms and kissed her madly.

Chapter Eleven

After most of the eating was finished, everyone assembled in the family room as they usually did, to play board games, chat and occasionally do a sing-along, which was always hysterical because none of them could carry a note. With a full belly, a room filled with people he loved and a sprinkling of laughter, Mark was in his element.

He sat back in his chair and watched Roni interacting with everyone as though she was perfectly at home. Her relationship with Luke was especially remarkable. It was clear the two connected on a deep level. He could see it in her eyes when she laughed at his jokes, in his expression when he looked at her.

Since he'd returned from the Marines, Luke had been a different person. Wounded and broken. The whole family had noticed. They'd all tried to reach out to the Luke they'd once known, but he'd locked himself away. Nothing had been able to bring him back.

Now, with Roni, Mark could see little flashes of his brother emerge. Could see the spark of joy in his eyes. Could feel his contentment as the two of them riffed about a show they both loved on Netflix. When the two of them burst into an off-key theme song and dissolved into laughter, something swelled in the general region of his chest.

He'd never seen his brother so animated. Never seen him laugh so much, open up like this. At least, not since he returned.

Roni caught his eye and made her way back to him, then perched on the arm of his chair. "How are you doing?" she asked. "Do you want more pie?"

He had to groan. "I'm stuffed."

"There's more."

"If I eat another bite I'm gonna pop a seam." She chuckled and then bent down to give him a kiss.

"Hey," Sam said, as though this kiss had reminded her she wanted to pry about something. "Have you two set a date?"

He blinked. "A date? We just decided—"

"You need to set a date."

Lizzie nodded. "You do. We have a wedding to plan."

Sam nodded. "A big wedding."

"Yay!" Emma took this opportunity to jump on the sofa. Her mother, in response, took this opportunity to tell her to stop. Emma made a face, but complied. The next words out of her mouth, though, made Mark wish she'd kept bouncing. "When are you going to have a baby?"

Silence fell after Lizzie scolded, *"Emma Jean!"*

Roni glanced at Mark with a wince.

"What?" Leave it to Sam to suss out the only fly in the proverbial ointment. "What's wrong?"

Mark put his arm around Roni's shoulder and pulled her closer. "Um, we've decided to take our time on that."

"Oh." The weight of it all was utterly lost on Emma, who went back to surreptitiously braiding the fringe on one of the pillows.

"Well, don't take too long. We need more kids around here," Sam insisted.

Lizzie nodded. "Emma needs playmates."

"Well, she has one coming," Roni said, waving to Lizzie's midsection. She then artfully shifted the conversation to Lizzie's pregnancy, which, to be frank, Lizzie was always willing to talk about.

Mark knew having a child was going to be a rough road for both of them. But he was determined to stick with it, no matter what. He would do whatever it took to make Roni's dreams come true. She deserved it.

As the chatter continued, Mark looked up at Roni. "You okay?" he whispered.

She slid down onto his lap, then put her arms around his neck and kissed him softly. "I am okay," she said, gazing into his eyes. "I am very okay."

Later, when Mark went to grab another beer, Emma crawled into Roni's lap; she just opened up her arms and let the little girl cuddle in. When it was bedtime, Lizzie suggested—and Emma insisted—that Roni tuck her in. Of course, *tuck her in* was really code for *read her to sleep*, apparently, because Roni didn't get halfway through the story. After she heard the little girl snore, she remained there, on her bed, just enjoying the warm bundle next to her. Enjoying the scent of innocence. It hardly broke her heart at all.

She looked up, tears in her eyes, and locked gazes with Mark, who was standing there, leaning against the jamb, watching her. He smiled. It was such a sweet, precious smile, some rare brand of great joy filled her chest.

This. This moment.

This was what she had been searching for. A man who was gentle, a man who protected and loved her. A child who needed her and adored her. This was what she'd always wanted. What she'd ached for. What she'd always ached for. For the first time in a very long time, she not only felt hopeful, but she also felt anticipation and it was delicious.

After a while, she untangled from Emma, kissed her on the forehead and headed back downstairs, hand in hand with Mark. He joined his brothers in front of the TV to watch football and Roni wandered into the kitchen, where Lizzie and Sam were doing the dishes. When she volunteered to help, they said she didn't have to, because she was a guest.

"Not anymore," she said with a grin. "Now I'm family," she said as she snapped on her rubber gloves.

"Okay," Sam said. "Whatever floats your boat."

"I'll wash, you dry and Lizzie will put away. How's that?"

"Why are you smiling?" Sam asked. "It's the dishes."

Roni sighed. "I've always enjoyed doing the dishes."

"Really?" Lizzie gaped.

"It's so…calming, I guess. Besides, this is such a normal, wonderful, holiday family thing to do." It was also a chance to talk with Sam and Lizzie. She'd decided that it would be easier for her if they both understood the reason she and Mark wouldn't make any babies. This was the perfect time to bring it up.

She waited until they'd finished the crystal glasses, just as a matter of courtesy. "You know," she said, as she started on the plates, "I wanted to talk to you guys in private about this—"

"Oh, my God. This sounds like bad news," Sam said.

Roni smiled sadly. "It's about why Mark and I won't be having kids right away. I just think you should know."

They both sobered.

Roni swallowed heavily. "I'm…not able to carry a baby." There. That was a good way to put it. Wasn't it?

"I'm so sorry, hon," Lizzie said as she folded her into a hug.

"Thank you, Lizzie."

She pulled back and set a hand on her belly. "Oh, gosh. I hope I haven't ever said anything that's made you uncomfortable."

What? Roni had to laugh. "Lizzie, I am delighted for you. How could I not be thrilled for you?"

Lizzie hugged her again. "That's just because you're such a wonderful soul. But if I ever start to kvell over baby stuff, kick me under the table, okay."

"I'll keep that in mind."

When Roni turned to Sam, she was frowning. "How do you know?" she asked.

Roni shrugged. "Because the doctors said so."

"Yeah, but how do you know for *sure*."

"Ah, it was a lot of doctors."

"You should still go for tests," Sam said. "I have a friend who was told she couldn't have kids, and she went to see this doctor in Kennewick. You know, at a fertility clinic. She ended up with triplets."

Lizzie made a face. "Oh, Lord. Triplets?"

"Mark and I are going to start looking into our options."

Lizzie nodded. "There are so many options these days. Medicine is amazing." She gave Roni another hug. "What do you say we leave the pots and pans for the men?" she said.

Sam tossed her towel onto the counter. "And this year, they won't just take them outside and squirt them with the hose."

For Mark, having his family approve of his engagement to Roni made it more real. A silly thought, because he would have married her even if they hadn't approved, but there you have it.

Now it was official.

Though she said she didn't care about a ring, he did, so he made plans to take her to Spokane to pick one out. They stayed overnight at the Historic Davenport Hotel, which was over a hundred years old and had been elegantly restored. Their room seemed to belong in a castle somewhere in Europe. While Roni oohed and aahed over the antique furniture and period hardware, Mark enjoyed the food. They both enjoyed the bed. Roni joked that the trip was like a pre-wedding honeymoon.

After they had the ring, an official announcement seemed logical. Butterscotch Ridge was a small town, so engagements were a big deal.

When they got back, he took her to the B&G for a quick bite and to discuss how they wanted to release their big news, only to discover that his friends were there. There wasn't a better way to get the word out than to tell them.

"Well, howdy, stranger!" Adam hollered, waving widely to be sure Mark saw him. As though he could miss him somehow.

"Where have you been?" Nadler asked in a petulant tone, before he nodded to Roni. They'd met when she was working to finance her bakery. In fact, all of his friends had met her at one point or another. Just not all at once like this.

For a second, he regretted stopping at the B&G. He should have taken her straight home.

"Where *have* you been?" Cole echoed. "I haven't seen you since…" He stopped short and glanced at Roni. "You doing all right, ma'am?" he asked.

Mark nearly burst into a guffaw at Roni's expression. Apparently she didn't care to be called ma'am.

Nadler pushed between them. "Since what?"

Mark put his arm around Roni and answered Cole. "She's doing fine." And apparently when he and Roni shared a smile at that, the others got suspicious.

"Why are you smiling like that?" Nadler asked.

Before they could respond, if they even intended to, Crystal came up with a tray of drinks for the guys. "Oh, my goodness," she said, setting down the tray and grinning at Roni. "Is that what I think it is?" she asked.

"What?" Nadler again.

Roni flushed and held out her hand. "It is."

She squealed and gave Roni a hug and then demanded to get a closer look.

His friends, on the other hand, stared at Mark in shock. After a moment, he decided he should probably say something. "Hey, guys, Roni and I are getting married."

"Married?" They all parroted in concert.

"How'd that happen?" Nadler asked.

"But you're supposed to be our only single friend," Adam said. "Where are we gonna hold our poker games?"

"Well, I'm happy for you." Cole thrust his hand out. "Even though I thought I'd never see the day. Roni is an amazing woman. Too good for you, in fact, man."

Adam snorted. "You're just saying that so she'll give you free cupcakes at the bakery."

"Hmm." Cole tapped his lip. "Would that work?" he asked her.

Her grin was cheeky. "Probably."

"Well, then, welcome to the family." He pulled Roni into a big hug before Mark could stop him, but for some reason, she didn't flinch. He liked the idea that she was becoming used to being hugged again. He didn't even mention that Cole wasn't part of the family.

He was part of the tribe, though, and that counted, too.

"Seriously," Adam said, though the grin on his face was obvious. "Where are we going to play poker?"

"Well," Roni said, "I'm not going to keep Mark from playing poker with his buddies."

"Do you play?" Nadler asked.

She shrugged. "I know how, but I don't play very well."

"Excellent," Adam responded with a mischievous glint in his eye. "That is excellent."

Roni should have been overwhelmed by everyone's response to the engagement, but they were all so kind and warm. It seemed as though she'd carved her place in this town after all.

When you belonged somewhere, it seemed, you didn't mind so much when people got into your business.

Sam, for instance, helped them find a fertility clinic in Kennewick.

As Roni and Mark made the long drive into the Tri-Cities for that appointment, Roni couldn't help remembering the time he'd taken her into town for supplies, and she'd ended up in his bed. Or he'd ended up in hers. Whatever. It was a good memory.

"What are you smiling about?" he asked.

"Nothing." But her grin widened. "I'm just happy."

"Are you?" He reached across the bench seat and took her hand. "I'm happy, too."

She gusted a sigh. "Might as well enjoy it. You know, the time when all things are possible. Before they tell us it's not."

"Keep an open mind," he reminded her. "We agreed to keep an open mind—"

"And be positive." She finished the sentence for him. "I'm trying."

He shot her a glance. "It is what it is. I'll always love you."

"And I'll always love you."

But what they both desperately wanted was someone else to love. Some small bundle of life to fill their hearts. Why did something that simple have to be so hard?

As Roni expected, after the tests, the doctors concurred that, while she did have viable eggs on one side, both fallopian tubes and one ovary were damaged and she'd suffered severe uterine scarring. Her chances of getting pregnant were between slim and none. And if she did get pregnant, the fetus would probably not attach. And if it did, the likelihood that it would go full term was almost nothing.

Roni sat there and listened, holding on to Mark's hand, and tried to fight back her emotions.

She knew all this. She'd known for a long time. It was silly to think some miracle had occurred just because she'd found the man of her dreams. Just because she wanted this so bad. Life didn't play out that way. It never did.

They went on, the clinicians, talking about surrogacy, about how they could harvest Roni's eggs and Mark's sperm and implant the embryo in someone else's womb. And they talked about how much that would be. The cost was astronomical.

Mark listened to every word, took all the literature they passed to him and asked questions as though any of this was feasible. Roni loved that about him. He was dogged and determined.

If he hadn't been, it would have been far too easy for her to give up on hope.

"That went well," he said as he started up the truck for the trek home.

She stared at him. "You call that good?"

He glanced at her and grinned. "Hon, weren't you listening? We have a real chance of having a baby."

Seriously? "Is that what you heard?" Had they been in the same room?

"He said you have viable eggs. All we need is a surrogate—"

"And thousands of dollars. Did you hear that part?"

He snorted. "I don't care how much it costs. We can do this."

"How can you say you don't care how much it costs?" Everyone cared about money.

His smile held a hint of smugness. "I have a job, you know. I get paid."

"Still—"

"And I don't have a lot of expenses. A couple beers a week. A monthly poker game. Car insurance, dog food… Yeah. I spend a bit on that, I guess—"

"What are you saying?"

He shrugged. "I have money in savings."

She frowned at him. "Not that much."

For some incalculable reason, he shrugged. "Don't worry about the money."

Don't worry about the money? If it had been a thousand dollars, even ten thousand, fifty thousand maybe, she could see it. But a hundred grand? Unthinkable.

"I don't know." She turned to stare out the window. "Our baby? Growing inside a stranger? It doesn't feel right."

He patted her hand, but kept his attention on the road. "People do it all the time. We could have her stay at the ranch with us. We can be a part of the pregnancy." He glanced at her then, and saw. He pulled over to the side of the road and took her in his arms. "Why are you crying, honey?"

So many excuses flooded her mind. There were so many reasons she could toss at him, so many ways to end this conversation. For some reason, she opted for the truth, as hard as it was to say. Mark deserved it. He'd earned it, in her eyes. She buried her face in his shoulder and whispered in his ear, "I just wish… I just wish he hadn't stolen everything from me. I wish I still felt like a whole woman. A real woman."

He pulled her closer and locked his gaze with

hers. "Roni, you *are* a real woman. You're as real as it gets."

The sincerity and adoration in his tone made it impossible for her heart not to melt. Her lips quirked upward as he blinked back the dampness in his eyes.

When he saw that, he smiled, too, with a hint of relief. He kissed her for a long time, there by the side of the road. He kissed her until she admitted she was feeling better.

It was even almost true.

Once the Stirling family got ahold of a bone, they never let go. Mark knew it, Hell, he'd lived with them his whole life, but he'd never seen anything like this. The frenzy with which they attacked plans for his wedding was downright rabid.

It was probably Sam's fault. She probably figured if they didn't get this thing done, and quick, he'd try to weasel out of it.

She couldn't have been more wrong.

It was more likely that Roni would change her mind. Yeah, so Mark didn't mind the rush.

What he did mind was the endless planning meetings the women insisted on. And, they insisted *he* be a part of them. Each and every one.

Because, really? Who cared what color the linens were? Or where the flowers were placed? Or whether they offered chicken or fish? Because beef was a given. Mark couldn't have cared less about seating charts and monkey suits and all that other nonsense everyone else seemed to be obsessed with. All he wanted was Roni.

"Just be patient," she said to him when he brought it up a couple weeks after they'd shared the news with his family. They sat in the parlor with cake samples all over the coffee table—the only part of this mess he'd actually enjoyed. "You know how long Sam has been dreaming of getting a brother married off. Let her have her fun."

Mark frowned at her. "*Danny's* married."

"I know. But she says that doesn't count because he's a *new* brother."

"You can't qualify things like that!"

Roni grinned. "You tell Sam that."

"Tell Sam what?"

Crap.

They both turned to the door. Both forced a smile. Or, at least, Mark did.

Roni's smile was probably real. She was sweet like that. "I was just telling Mark to be patient with all this wedding stuff."

Sam glanced at the table. "You complaining about cake tasting?"

"Not that. It's just… Well, all this nonsense, all this hullabaloo… It's not me."

His sister threw herself into an easy chair. "Well, this mess isn't for you. It's for Roni."

"For me?" Roni squeaked. "I'd be happy eloping."

Mark nodded. “Let’s do that, then.”

Sam glowered. “You didn’t let me finish. *And* it’s for the family, your friends, too. We deserve it.”

“If you want a party, just—”

“It’s not about the party, doofus. A big wedding is a statement.”

“What? That we can afford it?”

“No.” Sam blew out an impatient breath. “It’s not that at all, dummy. It’s a chance for everyone who loves you to celebrate you. That makes *them* feel good. You gonna steal that from them? From Cole or Adam?” She glanced pointedly at Roni. “Or Luke? Do you know how over the moon he is for you two? It’s almost like he had a part in getting you together.”

Maybe he had.

Sam barreled on. “You owe us.”

“She’s right.” Roni took Mark’s hand and squeezed.

“Damn straight, I’m right.” She waggled her finger at her brother. “Don’t you even think about eloping, or I might just change my mind about being your surrogate.”

Mark’s heart jerked. Roni dropped her fork.

They both gaped at Sam, sprawled as she was, all over the La-Z-Boy.

“What?” The word barely made it out of Mark’s throat. Something snagged it in there.

“Yeah.” She sat up straighter. “I decided to carry your baby. You know. If you want.”

"Sam." Roni stared at her, tears in her eyes. "That is so generous. But—"

"But nothing. I've always wanted to bring a child into the world, but my love life being what it is… well, this may be the only chance I get to feel all the ecstasies of pregnancy. Besides, paying a surrogate is the most expensive part of the procedure. This only makes sense. You need a womb. I have one. And, well, I am offering it to you."

"You'd be giving birth to your brother's kid…" Mark hated reminding her, but it needed to be said.

Sam shook her head. "I'd be giving my brother—and my dear friend—a kid. A kid they both want desperately. Look, I've thought this through. I want to do this. Think of it as a wedding present, okay?"

"Sam—"

She cut him off with the slash of a hand. "You guys set an appointment with the doctor and I'll be there. Now…" She eyed the cakes on the table. "Which one should I try first? Because we all know, once I'm carrying a baby, Lizzie's not going to let me taste sugar ever again."

And, since Mark knew his sister, and how she got once she made up her mind, he couldn't continue to argue. Frankly, it was a waste of time. Besides, he was too overwhelmed with love and gratitude to try. All he could manage was a hug. And then, he didn't want to let her go.

* * *

Funny how one kind act could change everything, especially a person's outlook. After that conversation, where Sam made that unbelievably generous gesture, some latent weight lifted from Roni's shoulders. She hadn't realized it was there until it disappeared.

Just having the option of Sam as a surrogate seemed to open doors, windows, moonroofs in Roni's mind. She *knew* she and Mark would have children. She could visualize herself being a mama. Imagine holding her baby in her arms. Smell the scent of his downy hair. Or hers.

Maybe that was why she was so giddy nowadays. That, and Mark's presence in her life. And the success of her bakery. And the fact that Gram had perked up significantly now that there was something for her to do all day. The future was bright, which filled Roni with gratitude and a kind of spiritual humility. To those who are given much, much is expected. And all she wanted to do now was give back as much as she could, and with joy.

Despite how long it seemed in coming, the day of the wedding dawned sooner than Roni anticipated. It felt as though she'd been sucked into a time warp that spat her out in the Butterscotch Ridge Unitarian Church in a wedding dress. Oh, she still remembered everything that had happened in the interim—and a lot had happened—but it seemed as though she'd witnessed it from a distance.

Even the day she and Mark had gone in to have her eggs harvested. The day they'd been implanted in Sam's womb.

Especially the day she'd gone to court to attest to the fact that Anthony had violated his restraining order. All the Stirlings went with her on that one.

There'd been some disappointments, too, like the news that her father couldn't get away from work to attend her wedding. She'd expected as much, though. She knew her father well enough. His career had always come first. There was no changing that.

Thank God, there was more than one kind of family; there was the family you were born with and the family you chose. And this was the one *she* had picked. She was sad her father couldn't get away, but her cup was full, anyway, and she knew it.

She'd also been super busy with the bakery in that time, keeping up with orders and teaching Carlos and Lupe all her recipes, so they could cover the store while she was on her honeymoon and—she hoped—after that. Now that she and Mark were on the way to parenthood, she'd need someone else running the day-to-day of the bakery, and Carlos and Lupe were an excellent addition to the team. They'd both worked at a bakery before and Lupe's cake decorating skills far surpassed Roni's. They were thankful for the work, but were over the moon when Roni and Mark decided that she and Gram should move to the ranch and were going to give them the apartment over the store.

The only downside was that Mark had to finally find new homes for the dogs. Gram wasn't steady on her feet on most days, and having five to seven dogs romping through the living room didn't help.

They did, however, keep Tallulah Belle and Snoopy. The puppers didn't go far. They were adopted by several ranch hands, and of course, Daisy went to Emma as promised. Mark was thrilled that they stayed close.

Ah, yes, it had been a busy time, but now, here she stood, at the back of the town's church, staring down the aisle at a beautiful sight: Mark Stirling, her handsome soon-to-be-husband, in an actual tuxedo. Damn, he looked good. But then, he looked good in a worn-out flannel work shirt. He looked especially good in nothing at all.

DJ stood beside him as his best man, and Cole, Adam and Nadler stood by his side. Emma, who had already strewn flowers along the path, peeped around the chair in the first row to watch Lizzie, Sam and Crystal make their way down the aisle to their places on the bride's side. Silence fell as the last of the wedding party took their places.

The crowd rustled, just a little, impatient perhaps, to see their local playboy finally take his vows. And then, when the wedding march rose—exquisitely, from a single violin—everyone stood and turned.

Roni was oblivious to all their stares. She was aware only of Mark staring at her with love in his eyes and conviction in his heart.

It was a beautiful thing, surrendering to love. There was such peace in it. She knew, because she felt it, too. She'd embraced it, too. She'd given up all the pain and anger and bitterness—for this. For him. It felt so right, this moment, so beautiful, it made her chest ache with joy and gratitude.

"You ready?" Luke asked, thrusting his elbow in her direction. It only made sense for him to give her away, given how close they'd become. He was sharp and stunning in his dress uniform, featuring his Purple Heart.

Her stomach fluttered as her pulse shot up. Was she ready? She glanced up at Luke and smiled. No woman had ever been so ready. "Onward," she said.

And then she took the first step toward the man she loved, and their new life together.

* * * * *

Look for Luke's story, the next installment of
New York Times *bestselling author*
Sabrina York's new miniseries

The Stirling Ranch
on sale February 2022
wherever Harlequin books and ebooks are sold.

And catch up with the Stirling siblings!

Don't miss
Accidental Homecoming*,*
Danny and Lizzie's story,
available now!

COMING NEXT MONTH FROM

HARLEQUIN

SPECIAL EDITION

#2869 THE FATHER OF HER SONS

Wild Rose Sisters • by Christine Rimmer

Easton Wright now wants to be part of his sons' lives—with the woman he fell hard for during a weeklong fling. Payton Dahl doesn't want her sons to grow up fatherless like she did, but can she risk trusting Easton when she's been burned in the past?

#2870 A KISS AT THE MISTLETOE RODEO

Montana Mavericks: The Real Cowboys of Bronco Heights
by Kathy Douglass

During a rare hometown visit to Bronco for a holiday competition, rodeo superstar Geoff Burris is sidelined by an injury—and meets Stephanie Brandt. Geoff is captivated by the no-nonsense introvert. He'd never planned to put down roots, but when Stephanie is in his arms, all he can think about is forever...

#2871 TWELVE DATES OF CHRISTMAS

Sutter Creek, Montana • by Laurel Greer

When a local wilderness lodge almost cancels its Twelve Days of Christmas festival, Emma Halloran leaps at the chance to convince the owners of her vision for the business. But Luke Emerson has his own plans. As they work together, Luke and Emma are increasingly drawn to each other. Can these utter opposites unite over their shared passion this Christmas?

#2872 HIS BABY NO MATTER WHAT

Dawson Family Ranch • by Melissa Senate

Nothing will change how much Colt Dawson loves his baby boy. Not even the shocking news his deceased wife lied about Ryder's paternity. But confronting Ava Guthrie about his ex's sperm-donor scheme doesn't go as planned. Will Ava heal Colt's betrayed heart in time for a Wyoming family Christmas?

#2873 THE BEST MAN IN TEXAS

Forever, Texas • by Marie Ferrarella

Jason Eastwood and Adelyn Montenegro may have hit it off at a wedding, but neither of them is looking for love, not when they have careers and lives to establish. Still, as they work together to build the hospital that's meaningful to them both, the pull between them becomes hard to resist. Will they be able to put their preconceived ideas about relationships aside, or will she let the best man slip away?

#2874 THE COWBOY'S CHRISTMAS RETREAT

Top Dog Dude Ranch • by Catherine Mann

Riley Stewart has been jilted. He needs an understanding shoulder, so Riley invites his best friend, Lucy Snyder, and her son on his "honeymoon." But moonlit walks, romantic fires, the glow of Christmas lights—everything is conspiring against their "just friends" resolve. Will this fake honeymoon ignite the real spark Riley and Lucy have denied for so long?

Nothing will change how much Colt Dawson loves his baby boy. Not even the shocking news his deceased wife lied about Ryder's paternity. But confronting Ava Guthrie about his ex's sperm-donor scheme doesn't go as planned. Will Ava heal Colt's betrayed heart in time for a Wyoming family Christmas?

Read on for a sneak peek at
His Baby No Matter What,
the next book in the Dawson Family Ranch miniseries by Melissa Senate!

"I wasn't planning on getting one," Ava said. "I figured it would be make me feel sad, celebrating all alone out at the ranch. My parents gone too young. And this year, my great-aunt gone before I even knew her. My best friend after the worst argument I've ever had. I love Christmas, but this is a weird one."

"Yeah, it is. And you're not alone. I'm here. Ryder's here. And like you said, you love Christmas. That house needs some serious cheering up. I want to get you a tree as a gift from me to you for our good deal."

"It *is* a good deal," she said. "Okay. A tree. I have a box of ornaments that I brought over in the move to the ranch."

He pulled out his phone, did some googling and found a Christmas-tree farm that also sold wreaths just ten minutes from here. He held up the site. “Let’s go after Ryder’s nap. While he’s asleep, we can have that meeting—I mean, *talk*—about our arrangement. Set the agenda. The… What would you call it in noncorporate speak?”

She laughed. “Maybe it is a little nice having a CEO around here,” she said, then took a bite of her sandwich. “You get things done, Colt Dawson.”

He reached over and touched her hand and she squeezed it. Again he was struck by how close he felt to her. But he had to remember he was leaving in two and a half weeks, going back to Bear Ridge, back to his life. There was a 5 percent chance, probably less, that he’d ever leave Godfrey and Dawson. But he’d have this break, this Christmas with his son, on this alpaca ranch.

With a woman who made him think of reaching for the stars, even if he wouldn’t.